Other Titles by Julia Jarman

HANGMAN

JULIA JARMAN

Andersen Press · London

First published in 1999 by
Andersen Press Limited,
20 Vauxhall Bridge Road, London SW1V 2SA

British Library Cataloguing in Publication Data available
ISBN 0 86264 866 1

Typeset by FSH, London WC1
Printed and bound in Great Britain by Mackays of Chatham PLC,
Chatham, Kent

1

It was a Saturday morning when Toby first heard the news. He'd just come in from football and was soaking wet, because it had rained all the way home. His mother was on the phone. 'Danny's coming to Lindley,' she mouthed. Then she covered the mouthpiece and said it aloud, thinking he hadn't understood first time, because he hadn't replied. He just carried on taking off his boots. He felt as if she'd just pointed to a fifty kilo weight and said, 'Pick that up, dear.' Suddenly the warm basement kitchen was less welcoming. The pan on the bright red stove hissed.

His mother said, ''Bye' – presumably to Danny's mother – and put down the phone, as Toby put a towel over his head and rubbed his wet hair.

'The pressure at Park House was too much for him,' his mum went on, ladling soup into yellow bowls. 'Poor Danny, he couldn't cope.' Smoke, the cat, rubbed against her trouser legs as she sat down at the pine table.

Park House was a private school where Danny had gone two years ago – when he was nine – to Toby's intense relief. For weeks his parents had agonised about moving him from All Saints Primary where both boys went. They'd involved Toby's mum and dad in their discussions. Then finally, they'd decided on Park House. Toby had laughed when Danny showed him the prospectus. The teachers looked like something out of the Beano. Danny loved it though, right from the start: the masters in Batman gowns – it was a boys only school – the purple-striped uniform with a daft cap, all the daft rules about stupid things. Danny had loved it all.

'Toby!' called his mum as he headed for the door.

'I'm not hungry! I'm going to get changed!'

Danny coming to Lindley High was bad news. Danny coming to Lindley was dire.

'Hang on! You must be hungry. Take this upstairs if you like.' She put the soup and some bread on a tray, while he waited.

'Elsa said he's starting on Monday, and would you look out for him.'

Worse and worse.

Too soon. Too late. Typically Danny. They were nearly two weeks into the term already. Starting a school mid-term was bad for anyone. For someone like Danny it could be fatal.

'He's going to be in 7Y.'

Toby breathed more freely. He was in 7X. The forms didn't mix that much.

'Elsa said she tried to get him in 7X, but there are over thirty already or something. An imbalance. Anyway, she's asked Nick Tate's mother if Danny can go with him on his first day. Nick's in 7Y and the Tates live in the same road.'

Even better. Nick Tate was one of those well-respected types. He played in all the school teams, was on the school council. Teachers loved him. If Nick took

Danny under his wing he might be okay. If . . . Not many people took to Danny. That was the trouble.

'Elsa says she hopes you won't mind, about her asking Nick I mean.'

Toby nearly laughed at that. Elsa Lamb was stupid. He was amazed that she was his mum's best friend. They were complete opposites in looks and character. Gilly Peters had dark curly hair and was on the cuddly side; Elsa was pale and spiky and Elsa went *on*.

'She said you're the main reason Danny wants to go to Lindley. You were such a help to him at All Saints. Well, at least you'll see each other in the playground.'

Not if I can help it.

Toby took the tray from her. It was definitely time to go upstairs. Any second now his head would be a red blob as skin and freckles merged with his hair. He could feel himself getting hotter as memories of the playground came flooding back.

Of Danny's ineptness at football, for instance, so no one wanted to play with him.

Of Danny's ineptness at any ball game.

Of Danny playing hopscotch with the girls.

Of Danny in PE asking to be his partner. He never asked anyone else.

Of feeling bad because you refused.

Of feeling bad because you agreed. There was no winning with Danny.

Why? *Why* did he have to come to Lindley?

As Toby climbed the upper staircase he could see his attic

3

bedroom through the open door; and a dusty box of Lego under his bunk bed. It reminded him that he and Danny had got on well once, when they were little. Their families had been friends so they'd grown up together. They used to dig in the garden side by side, and ride their little bikes, stuff like that – and go swimming. Their families had met at Sunday morning swimming lessons and used to have brunch together afterwards. Danny had been okay at swimming. Their families matched in a way. They both lived in big Victorian houses on the outskirts of Allton – though quite far apart – and they had similar interests. And Danny and Toby both had younger sisters who were friends too. It was only when they started school that Toby noticed that Danny was different. Then it became all too obvious and he wondered why he hadn't noticed before. Danny didn't look like other kids looked, though it was hard to say what the difference was, and he didn't like what other kids liked – pop music for instance. He loved Classic FM. Well, so did Toby sometimes, at home with his family. But he didn't talk about it and Danny did. That was another thing – he didn't know when to keep quiet. When the others talked about pop music, he'd say, 'It's not really to my taste.' He didn't even *talk* like anyone else.

Toby climbed to the top of his bunk-bed, got a book from under his pillow and tried to forget Danny. But memories kept coming back, how once he'd gone on for weeks about Beethoven. He got crazes. Not that he was any good at music. He couldn't even keep time. In class if they were clapping to music, or beating time with percussion instruments, they'd come to the end. Silence. Then – CRASH! – Danny, after everyone else had finished! That summed it up in a way. Everyone used to laugh, till the teacher stopped them because Danny got so upset. Toby had got upset too – for Danny. *That's* what he didn't want to start again either. He pulled the duvet over his head. He couldn't bear that again.

He wouldn't bear it.

Far below a doorbell rang. Must be Polly back from dancing classes. With Jess, Danny's little sister, probably. Polly and Jess were best friends when they weren't worst enemies. They were both bossy. Jess was a right little Hitler in fact, not a bit like Danny. Danny was stupidly obedient. If you told him to put his head in the fire he'd do it. Toby got out of bed and closed his bedroom door. He needed to be on his own.

'You *what*?'

On the other side of Allton, Nick Tate couldn't believe what his mother was saying. He'd just come in from football too, but was already sitting at the table in clean jeans and sweat shirt. Nick was captain of Lindley's junior team and their best player.

His mother ran her fingers through her hair and sounded exasperated.

'It's just for his first day, Nick. Finish laying the table will you, please.'

'Too right it is! I'll go on my bike.' Nick stomped off to the cutlery drawer and met his father coming from his study.

'What's this?' Alec Tate arranged his long legs round the chrome table legs and put a book by his plate. It was called *The Criminal Gene – Fact or Fiction?*

Beth Tate sighed as she put salad and quiche in front of them both.

'I've agreed to give Danny Lamb a lift to school on Monday. The boy's new. The family live up the road. His mother asked me, and Nick objects.'

'Why, Nick?' His father peered over his half-glasses.

'Because he's a prat.'

'Do you know him?'

'I've seen him. He's got girlie hair and he wears a stupid uniform.'

'Do you know him?'

'No.'

'Well, you're *pre-judging* the situation, aren't you? That's what prejudice is, Nick.'

Alec Tate was a police officer who never let you forget it, but he liked to think he was ultra-reasonable.

'Wait till you've met the boy before you make up your mind about him. Agreed?'

'Agreed.' There was no point in arguing.

'End of subject then. And don't give your mother hassle, right? What's this?' He poked the quiche with his fork.

Beth Tate looked as if she was going to say something, but decided against it and sat down.

His father patted Nick's close-cropped head. 'Would you say my hair was "girlie", Nick?'

Nick laughed. His dad had about three long strands

6

and a lot of bare skull, which was usually hidden under his inspector's hat.

Later, when his parents were out at an art exhibition, Nick rang his mate, Callum Nolan.

'Problem! My mum's said I'd show this weird kid round school on Monday. Danny Lamb. You don't know him – he went to a different primary – but you may have seen him. He lives in our road, the old part not our modern bit. It's not fair. She never even asked!'

Callum said he'd come round pronto. A few minutes later he was ringing the bell of the Tates' detached modern house, but Nick was already opening the door.

Toby had a shower and tried not to think about Danny. He kept telling himself – *he's not my responsibility. He isn't*. It wasn't as if Danny was thick. Nor was he one of those super-clever kids you heard about. He definitely wasn't a genius, though he was a bit of a swot in some ways. He'd got a bit behind in the Juniors though, mostly because there was a lot of free choice. He was hopeless at choosing; could never make up his mind whether to do his project or read a book or something else. So he'd just stand there dithering, till Toby decided for both of them. He didn't want that again either. He *wasn't* going to do that again.

While looking for something to wear, Toby found a photo of the Lambs and the Peters on holiday in Derbyshire, all with their arms round each other's shoulders. The two families sometimes went on walking holidays together. That one had been good. He and

Danny found some fossils for the museum they'd begun when they were little. When they were digging in the garden Danny used to wash the bits of pot or bone that they found. Then he'd label them and keep them tidy on a shelf in his room. That was another weird thing. He was very tidy and got stressed if things got moved from where he'd put them. Danny loved historical things, probably because his dad was into history. When the families were out walking they'd often end up in a graveyard, with Martin Lamb giving them a lecture on some bod buried there. He knew Latin and could translate the epitaphs on some of the older tombs. Occasionally it was interesting but Toby usually wandered off after a bit with Polly and Jess. But Danny loved listening to his dad. In fact he asked to learn Latin and even bought himself a Latin dictionary, with some money his granny sent him, so he could translate the epitaphs himself. And that was okay, Toby thought – it's a free country – *as long as he kept quiet about it* at school. But Danny didn't, of course. No wonder people thought he was weird.

That last holiday had been particularly good, Toby now realised, because he knew Danny wasn't coming back to All Saints in the September. Knowing that had been a big relief. Not having to defend Danny. Not having to befriend Danny. It would give him a chance to make other friends.

So he'd been pleased when Danny had been happy at Park House. He didn't mind seeing him occasionally, when the families met for Sunday lunch for instance.

But now what?

On Monday morning, when his mum gave him his packed lunch, she said, 'You will look out for Danny, won't you, Toby? You will be friendly?'

She was surprised that Toby hadn't rung Danny.

Toby was surprised that Danny hadn't rung him.

He'd thought it all out – I won't be *not* nice to him. I won't be *un*friendly. But I'm not going to be his best friend. He'd started to make new friends at Lindley, though he hadn't got a best mate yet. He'd had to make new friends, because he'd been put in 7X, when most kids he knew from All Saints had been put in 7Y. It wasn't streaming – or so the school said – but the Y class did seem to have most of the brains. So he'd felt a bit put out then – as if he wasn't bright enough for 7Y. Now, for the first time, he was pleased about it. If Danny was in a different class it shouldn't be too difficult to avoid him.

He saw the Tates' red Volvo go past as he turned into Lindley Road, walking carefully because the chestnut leaves underfoot were slippery, though it had stopped raining. There was a bit of a breeze and the sun was out. He caught a glimpse of Danny on the back seat of the Volvo and hoped Danny hadn't seen him.

2

Danny had seen him. It was the one good thing about the journey. His spirits rose when he recognised Toby among a group of Lindley pupils walking beneath the chestnut trees. All the pupils looked alike in their black blazers and grey trousers or skirts, but Toby's hair – the colour of the conkers on the ground – made him stand out. Nick Tate, in the front of the car by his mother, wasn't being at all friendly. Nor was the other boy, Callum Nolan, who was on the back seat with Danny. Neither of them had said anything, for the whole of the journey, but they were passing messages with their eyes. He could see them because Nick had pulled down the passenger seat mirror. Nick had blue eyes and Callum had grey eyes and their eyebrows went up and down.

Mrs Tate said, 'How are you feeling, Danny?'

And he said, 'A bit nervous.' Then wished he hadn't said it.

Callum sighed ever so loudly and Nick's eyebrows went up.

Mrs Tate didn't seem to notice how unfriendly they were. She said briskly, 'Oh, you'll be okay, won't he, lads? Lindley's a nice school. Friendly. I see a lot of schools and I can tell you, Lindley's one of the best.'

She explained that she was the school welfare officer,

so she knew all the schools in the area. Some of them were quite rough, she said, but Lindley had a good reputation. She looked like an officer with her grey suit and white shirt.

Danny couldn't help feeling nervous. He desperately wanted everything to go well on his first day, but hadn't known what lessons to prepare for. Should he have brought a PE kit? Should he have brought a lab coat like at Park House? Were calculators allowed? He still didn't know why things had gone wrong at Park House. For two years he'd loved it. Then suddenly the work got harder. His homework had taken him hours to do and then he'd got bad marks for it – and for the weekly tests. Then, he'd been asked to leave, just like that, without warning. The head had written to his parents saying he wasn't the 'right material'. He'd seen the letter, but still didn't know what that meant. Not the right material. He fingered the cuff of his blazer.

And Nick, watching Danny, saw him. He was doing what he'd promised his father, watching before he made up his mind. So far nothing had made him change his first opinion. What a prat.

'I'm nervous.' What a prat thing to say! Though he ought to be nervous looking like that. Calf eyes – big, brown and watery. Skin like raw pastry. And most people had a hair-style nowadays. Danny Lamb just had hair. Nick admired his own velvety skull in the mirror – and Callum's. They had identical cuts except for the Nike logo at the back of Callum's. His dad wouldn't allow that. He glanced again at Danny, leaning forward in his seat clutching his school bag. He obviously had no idea what *laid-back* meant. Hadn't he seen the streets of Lindley before?

He was an anorak. He even wore an anorak over his Lindley uniform. You could just see him collecting train numbers.

Suddenly, a Radio 4 voice said, 'Today's school bully has a four to one chance of being tomorrow's criminal or a captain of industry according to a leading psychologist. It depends...' But the rest was drowned by crackles. Mrs Tate said, 'Blast, that was interesting, I wanted to hear that,' as she fiddled with the controls. 'We have trouble with bullying in some schools.'

Callum mouthed 'Nerd', with a nod in Danny's direction and Nick grinned. Exactly. Nerd. Turd. Wally. Dickhead. All rolled into one. The sooner they dumped him the better. It would not do to be seen walking into the playground with him.

When Danny saw the sign saying LINDLEY ROAD he thought they must be nearly there. The traffic was heavier, with cars bringing pupils to school mostly and Mrs Tate had slowed down. Lindley High was a comprehensive with a good reputation, she said again. It had been the grammar school and people came to it from miles around. They were lucky to live in the leafy suburbs and not on one of the estates round Allton, she went on. Then she drew in suddenly, saying, 'I'd better drop you here, lads, or I'll be late.' They were by a beech tree in front of the driveway of a big house.

Nick and Callum got out and started walking ahead, but Danny's bag caught on the handbrake. Then the cord of his anorak got caught in the door.

Mrs Tate called out, 'Don't forget to show Danny the ropes, boys!'

Then Danny had to run after them, wishing he didn't need to. But he had to because he wasn't sure where the entrance was. He wished he could see Toby. Once he'd found Toby he wouldn't need these two.

They were walking even faster, now that Mrs Tate had driven off, and he had to stop to let a car into another driveway. It looked like a school entrance. He could see a brick doorway with white pillars on either side but there weren't any pupils going into it. But he couldn't see Nick and Callum now, either. Thinking he'd lost them, Danny kept on walking but Nick was waiting, leaning against a gatepost further up. Hundreds of pupils, some on bikes, were streaming through the gateway towards a more modern part of the school. Danny thought he might just follow them when Nick smiled and said, 'I'll show you the ropes, okay?'

So Danny smiled back and followed him along a gravel path towards a glass door in the side of the building, though no one else was going that way. Everyone else was going in the other direction. But Nick had opened the door and was holding it open, pointing inside. So Danny looked – into the gym – and saw that Nick was pointing to the ropes bunched at the side by the wall bars.

'Ropes,' he said. 'Go hang...?' He smiled again, but before Danny could smile back he sighed loudly and set off across the gym, motioning Danny to follow. So he did – through a door on the other side into a corridor where there was a flight of stone stairs leading to the first floor. And Nick stood there pointing to a rubber plant at the top.

'The form room,' he said. 'It's up there.' His words echoed in the empty building. Danny's heart thumped against his ribcage. He could feel it. Something wasn't right. He shouldn't be here. Where should he be? Why did he think so slowly? He must *decide* what to do. Why had Nick brought him here?

'Room 8. It's at the top of the stairs,' said Nick, tapping his foot against the stone step. The sound rang out and Danny still didn't move.

'The form teacher will be there,' Nick said. He spoke slowly and distinctly as if to someone thick. 'You can ask her about things.' Danny felt his palms go sweaty and stared at the rubber plant. Slow thinking – that was his trouble. That's why he'd been asked to leave Park House. He couldn't think fast enough. The weekly tests against the clock, even more than the mountains of homework, had beaten him.

Tap tap tap went Nick's foot.

Twenty spellings in a minute.

Tap tap tap.

Twenty mental arithmetic.

Tap tap tap.

Twenty French vocab.

He knew the answers, just couldn't think of them fast enough.

Nick started to climb the stairs. 'Come *on*!'

Danny followed. Past the rubber plant – and there was a corridor with lots of doors. Nick opened the first door and held it open, pressing his back against it.

'This is 7Y's room,' he said. 'Miss ----'ll be here soon.'

Danny didn't catch the teacher's name as he stepped inside.

'W-what does one do now?' he managed to say at last.

But Nick had gone, closing the door behind him. Hearing his receding footsteps, Danny hated himself for being so stupid. If only Toby were here.

Should he go and look for him? But he might get lost if he did. How long was it till the bell? It was a quarter to nine by his watch. Going with Nick had been a bad idea. Why hadn't he just followed all the others into the playground? *Why* didn't he think of things at the right time?

He looked round the classroom. What was the teacher's name? It must be here somewhere, but everything was in a muddle. The desks weren't in lines like at Park House. Some of them were pushed together. There were lots of things on the walls – multiplication tables and parts of speech, and the planets of the solar system and more planets hanging from the ceiling. Mars twizzled above the teacher's desk. Eventually he opened the door and found her name on the other side. Of course. Mrs Dempsey, that was it. He'd met her last week with his mum. She'd seemed nice, like his granny. He looked forward to seeing her.

But when the bell rang the teacher who came into the room wasn't Mrs Dempsey. This one was much younger with blonde hair like Jess's Barbie doll. When she came up the stairs with the rest of the class, she didn't notice him standing by the door. Nobody did. They just passed by him.

'Good morning, 7Y,' she said brightly.

'Good mor-ning, Mrs Pep-per,' they all droned and sat down.

So he was the only one standing up.

He could feel them all staring at him.

She said, 'Sit down, boy!'

But the only spare seat was in the middle of the room, near Nick and Callum.

A girl said, 'He's new, Miss.'

So was the teacher. She said, 'Sorry, yes, I have been told, it's er...' She consulted the register. 'Danny Lamb, isn't it? Well, Danny, I hope you'll be very happy at Lindley. Now there's a spare seat by Nick I think.'

But that chair had gone.

Mrs Pepper said, 'Come *on*. There was a spare chair.'

Someone laughed.

Someone else said, 'Baa Lamb!'

And Mrs Pepper said, 'Come *on*,' again.

Then the girl who'd said 'He's new' found the chair on its side at the back of the room. Carrying it back to her place, she said Danny could sit by her.

When he didn't move she said, 'Come here.' When he

did there were a lot of whistles and laughter.

A boy, with eyebrows that met in the middle, shouted, 'Be gentle with him, Louise!'

Mrs Pepper said, 'That's enough, Kevin. Thank you, Louise.'

Louise was tall with long, fair hair. Even sitting down she looked taller than anyone else in the class. She introduced Danny to a plump, dark girl called Rachel and the other girls in their group, but Danny didn't take in their names straightaway. One of them asked him how he grew his eyelashes so long. She said his eyes were nice. He thought her name was Patsy. Rachel had a brace on her top teeth. That's how he remembered her, and because, when Mrs Pepper gave him a copy of the timetable, she explained it. First lesson was Art, she said, a double lesson in the art room downstairs. They weren't streamed for Art so they all went to the same place. It was very confusing so he just followed her.

Two boys shoved past on the way down, but everyone else was okay. When they arrived in the art room, Mr Turtle, the teacher, was stapling something to a screen, and paused only to tell them to get on with what they'd started last week.

Louise said, 'Don't you think he looks a bit like a turtle? With his little head peeping out of that polo?'

She explained that they were supposed to be doing self-portraits in whatever medium they chose. Some people had brought in photographs to work from, she said, but there were mirrors to use. You could draw or paint, do a collage or work with clay. When he just stood there – because it was confusing – Rachel got him a mirror and some paper and charcoal and told him to draw himself.

It was really interesting, looking in the mirror. He had got long eyelashes. The boy called Kev pushed his chair once, but when Louise told him to get lost he went away. Quite a few people didn't seem to be doing much work. Kev didn't do any at all; he just went round annoying people. He'd push someone's elbow or kick their chair for no reason at all. Mr Turtle didn't seem to notice. Nick seemed to have disappeared.

In fact Nick was working in the store at the back of the art room. He tried to keep out of other kids' way in Art. It was one of the lessons they tended to mess around in. He didn't like messing around. It wasn't worth the risk. Things could get back to his father very quickly. Besides, he had a good idea and wanted to make it work. He wanted to make a model of himself as an athlete, but it was proving harder than it looked. He was trying to combine two images – a favourite photo of himself getting a medal for swimming, and a Greek statue of a discus thrower. But the brown clay kept falling off the wire frame he'd made.

It didn't help having that nerdish Danny Lamb in the room.

He persevered though and by the time the bell rang it was taking shape. The arms and legs looked muscular and strong. If he put a bit more on the chest he'd have a good likeness in his opinion. Thinking he'd ask Mr

Turtle if he could stay in at break and finish it, he went to find the teacher.

But when he came back there was Callum in the store, head on one side, grinning.

'Who's this then?' he said with his slightly Scottish accent. 'The seven stone weakling or Dopey the dwarf?'

Laughing, he moved round the table to look at Nick's model from another angle.

Then he said, 'Do you know what? Your athletic hero looks a bit like the new prat.'

He didn't say any more. He couldn't have said anything worse. Nick wasn't laughing. His eyes had clouded over. He'd seen it – that was the trouble – there was a resemblance.

Callum said, 'Come on, forget it. Let's go and have a game.'

But Nick picked up a bit of wire and began to stab the weakling's eyes out. Then he hurled the lot in the bin.

3

In the playground Danny looked for Toby and spotted him playing football. He didn't manage to speak to him though. He just couldn't seem to catch his eye. During the lunch hour he looked for him again, but couldn't find him anywhere.

Toby was keeping a low profile, even lower than he'd intended. When Callum came into the playground that morning saying a real nerd had joined the school, Toby guessed who and kept quiet. For about a second he considered being a hero saying, 'Danny's different, that's all, leave him alone.'

Then he'd had a flashback – of Danny in the junior playground pretending to be a butterfly. He'd kept out of Danny's way ever since. It wasn't that he wanted Danny to suffer. He didn't. He kept an eye on him, from a distance in the playground – and Danny looked okay. Some of the girls seemed to like him. He didn't *need* Toby. Talking to the girls at break didn't improve his standing with the boys, of course. There was a bit of name-calling. 'Big girl! Show us your tits!' – things like that but nothing serious. Even Kev Walsh left him alone. Kev, who had a go at most new kids, was more interested in playing football. There was a lot of competition to get in the school teams that term. Toby was trying hard to get in the Year-7 team.

He was behind Danny going home on a couple of occasions. Well, half-way home, because Danny had further to go, and that confirmed what he'd seen at school. Danny was okay. He was always by himself but he didn't look unhappy, just as if he was in a dream. He'd stop sometimes to stroke a cat or dog. Danny liked animals. He'd have loved a dog, but his mum didn't like them. He should have had a dog, an adoring Labrador or a huge St Bernard to look after him, Toby thought.

But Danny *was* unhappy. It wasn't long before Toby learned that. Danny wasn't happy at all. How many times did he hear that from his mum?

'Danny isn't happy, Tobe.'

'Elsa says Danny isn't happy at Lindley.'

'He says he never sees you.'

'I'm in a different class, that's why.'

'I don't like to nag, Tobe, but Elsa thinks if you walked home with him sometimes.'

'I have clubs.' It was true. He did have clubs or practices, three times a week.

'Or talked to him in the playground.'

Things did get worse for Danny in the playground. Toby saw that. But it was bound to. Kev Walsh couldn't hold off for long. The thing to do was stand up to him. Toby had had to do that in the first two weeks. Say, 'F--- off, Kev!' – and give him a shove.

Danny didn't, of course.

If only he'd been good at something that other people cared about. Or if he knew how to act. The football

21

crowd didn't let him play football naturally. So *why* did he start hanging around on the sidelines, as if he expected to be invited to play? The others started using him. If the ball went out of play, into the spinney or the ditch at the far side of the playground, then Kev or Nick or Callum would send Danny to fetch it. Then they sent him to fetch it when it *didn't* go out of play.

'It's gone into the spinney, Danny. After it, boy!'

And when he came back without it – 'Bad boy, Danny! Fetch bally! Go fetch!'

It got them lots of laughs. Of course, this didn't happen when teachers were looking. Toby *willed* Danny to say, 'No. F--- off!' Or just go away.

It was after school one Thursday, when Toby saw things take a turn for the worse. Danny must have been at Lindley for about two weeks. Toby happened to be going home after chess club which had ended early. He came out of a side entrance into Stockwood Road and there was Kev Walsh, on the opposite side, shouting. It was just beginning to get dark, and he was standing beneath a street lamp whose orange glow made his shaved head look like a Belisha beacon. His hands were cupped over his mouth.

'Dani-elle! Dani-elle!'

You didn't have to be a genius to guess who he was yelling at.

Danny was further up the road on the pavement, his way barred by a couple of other boys. It was hard to see who, because the beeches were casting shadows in the yellow light. But when a car went by, Toby recognised Callum Nolan and Froggy Lewis. And there was someone else near Kev, half hidden by the lamp post, saying something to him.

Toby felt that he should make his presence known, but he'd stopped walking and it wasn't easy to know when to start.

The person talking to Kev was Nick Tate.

'Dani-elle!' Kev yelled again. *'Danielle, parlee-voo france-say?'*

Danny must have been daft enough to show he was good at French in class.

'Dani-elle, do you smell?'

The others all held their noses and fell about laughing.

It looked as if Nick was making the bullets and Kev was firing them. Toby was surprised.

'Wee wee!' yelled Kev.

Then Nick and Kev started walking towards Danny, who just stood there with his head down. Toby started walking too,

Sticks and stones will break my bones,
But names they cannot hurt me.

That's what he hoped. He kicked the leaves as he went to be more noticeable. Surely they wouldn't do anything, not if they knew someone was watching? Nick Tate wasn't the sort. His father was a policeman who gave talks in school assemblies. Nick was well in with teachers. He talked as posh as they did, posher than some of them.

'Dani-elle, do you smell?' Kev didn't talk posh.

'Yes, you do! You're a poo!' The rest chanted as if they were at a football match.

'Flush him down the TOILET!'

Laughing, they'd surrounded Danny now, but he started to walk forwards. Good old Danny, Toby thought. It made Callum and Froggy Lewis and a third person – a tall, curly-haired dark boy called Big George – start to walk backwards down the street. They were all laughing, well all except Kev who seemed annoyed that he wasn't getting more reaction from Danny, who just kept his head down and put one foot in front of the other – even when Kev pulled the cord out of his anorak and threw a few leaves at him.

They carried on till they turned into Lindley Road and the traffic increased. Then they quietened down a bit, probably because there were more people about. And Toby, still following at a distance, saw Big George and Froggy Lewis cross the road and turn left into Elm Road. Some people called those two Little and Large.

In Beech Road, where Toby lived, Kev dropped Danny's anorak cord in the gutter. Toby picked it up. None of them saw him though.

He felt a bit bad when he turned into number forty-two, because Danny still had a ten-minute walk ahead of him, and so did Nick and Callum. He could see them following him. But his main feeling was relief – for several reasons.

The house was quiet. His mother must have taken Polly somewhere. Yes, there was a note on the table saying so. He stroked Smoke who was asleep on the

Aga, and made himself a drink.

After about ten minutes he rang the Lambs' number. Nobody answered. After another five he rang again. Someone picked up the phone, but put it down again.

Danny was in fact home and did hear it ringing. It was ringing as he came in the door, shaking so much he could hardly get the key in the lock. He didn't answer because he thought it might be one of his persecutors. When it kept ringing and he lifted up the receiver and heard Toby's voice, he put it down again. He went straight upstairs to his bedroom and closed the door. Then he tidied the collections on his shelves. He couldn't trust his voice.

Toby, taunting him.

For that's how it looked to him. He'd glanced back once and there was Toby with the others. Toby, his *first* friend. Toby his *best* friend – with Kev and Callum and Nick and some other boys. All the way home, that's what he'd thought of most. That's what had hurt him most. When the phone rang again he didn't hear it. He was far too busy.

Toby, at the other end of the phone, was worried.

Ten minutes later he rang again and kept ringing till at last Danny's mum answered it. She'd just come in the door, she said, and would hand the phone to Danny. She said he must be upstairs. He'd have answered if he'd been in the kitchen. As she climbed the stairs to Danny's room, Elsa said how glad she was that Danny and Toby were in touch again. In the background he heard Jess say, 'Tell Danny to feed Bunjy. It's his turn.'

Elsa said she was sure Danny would be okay if he had just one true friend.

When Toby got to speak to Danny he tried to give him some good advice. He said, 'You've got to stand up to them. Tell them to F-off. Say it. Swear. Use the same language they do. Stand up for yourself.'

But Danny didn't say anything. Danny couldn't say anything. He felt as if he didn't know Toby any more.

Afterwards he wondered why he didn't say, 'Why don't you stand up to them with me, instead of joining them? If standing up to them is such a good idea, two of us together would have more chance.'

Instead he let Toby talk. Toby went on for several minutes. Then he said, 'Danny? Danny? Are you there? I've got your anorak cord.'

But the line went dead.

Toby swore as he put down the phone. If Danny didn't want his advice, he'd save his breath. He'd tried to help. He'd done what he could. If Danny didn't want to talk about it, it was his own stupid fault. He'd have to cope with the consequences. He didn't have to come to Lindley. Nobody asked him to.

At supper Elsa Lamb said, 'That was nice of Toby to ring. What did he want?'

Danny didn't answer. He studied his dad's collection of old kitchen implements on the pine wall. It was too upsetting. The two mothers were best friends. What

26

would they say to each other if they knew he and Toby had broken their friendship? What would their fathers and sisters say? The families were friends still. The Peters were all coming for Sunday lunch soon, so his mum said.

When his mum asked what sort of day he'd had, he did say he'd been teased on the way home. And his dad, who was a gentle person – he and Danny looked a lot alike – said, 'Give as good as you get, son. If they punch you, punch them back.'

But his mum said, 'If you're not a puncher, Danny, don't punch.'

It was confusing. They said different things.

His mum said, 'Should I have a word with your teachers?'

But his dad said that might make things worse. He said he'd been bullied when he was a new boy at school. They'd moved from the north to the south and he'd had the wrong accent, but when he'd thumped the biggest bully it had stopped.

Jess said, 'I'd tell them to flop off and kick them in the goolies.' She would too. She looked all cute and girlie with her bows and bunches but she could be really fierce. Elsa told her to finish her moussaka quickly and go upstairs, but she didn't.

The talk of thumping made Danny feel even more nervous about school the next day. When he went to bed he read till he was nearly asleep, but when he put his book down he started worrying again. After he'd been lying in the dark for a while, Jess came into his room and asked him to read her a story. Climbing into his bed, she said she couldn't sleep either. She smelt nice – of talcum powder and toothpaste and she had one of their favourite stories, *Can't You Sleep, Little Bear?* It was about Big Bear who was a grown-up and Little Bear who was afraid of the dark – till he cuddled up to Big Bear who showed him the big yellow moon. Jess was a bit afraid of the dark. She switched on his bedside lamp and said, 'Read this to me, Dan, like when I was little.'

Near the end of the book there was a lovely picture of the two bears by the fire.

'What do they mean?' she said, pointing to some tiny words under a statue of a bear throwing a ball. The statue was on Big Bear's mantelpiece – and it was one of the reasons Danny liked the book too.

'URSUS MAJOR,' he said, and told her they meant Big Bear. 'Ursus' was Latin for 'bear' and 'major' was Latin for 'big'. 'And his book's called URSUS. Look,' he said.

She said, 'You *are* clever, Dan, and nice and gentle like Big Bear. I don't know why those boys are horrid to you.'

He said, 'You're horrid to me sometimes.'

She furrowed her brow. 'That's different. I'm your sister.'

He put out the light and she said, 'You're not afraid of the dark are you, Dan?'

He said, 'No.'

'What are you afraid of?'

'People,' he said, because it was true. He didn't understand people.

Light followed dark and dark followed light. But you never knew what people were going to do next. Soon he could hear the soft sound of Jess, sucking her thumb. Then he lay awake, with Jess cuddled up beside him, wishing he didn't have to go to school in the morning.

4

His mum took them both to school in her yellow 2CV, dropping Jess off at All Saints first. On the way Jess said, ' I've been thinking, Dan. You're too nice, like one of those stiff old-fashioned teddy bears. Perhaps you should be fiercer?' When she got out she said, 'Don't forget what I told you about kicking, Dan!'

His mum said, 'Jess!' but she'd already run off to join a crowd of her little friends. Jess had loads of friends even though she was bossy and selfish a lot of the time. When they got to Lindley High, his mother drew up behind the Tates' Volvo, though Danny asked her not to.

Mrs Tate shouted from the Volvo window, 'Any time Danny wants a lift, he's only got to ask!' Then she drove off. Nick had told her that Danny didn't want to come with them on a regular basis.

Danny waited till Nick and Callum were out of sight before he got out of his mum's car. But they were waiting for him round the comer. Nick stepped out from behind one of the huge trees. 'Bonjour, Danielle!'

'F--- off!'

They laughed. 'Who's a naughty girl then? Ooh la! You mustn't swear, Danielle. Nice girls don't swear!'

This went on till they reached the playground where Mr Hall was on duty. Then they became perfect pupils. Mr Hall was one of those teachers no one messed with.

He taught Maths.

'Good morning, Mr Hall.'

'Good morning, Nick. Callum . . . er?'

'It's Danny, Sir. New boy.'

'Thank you, Nick. How's your father?'

'All right, Sir. He's coming in next term to give a talk on drugs.'

Fortunately it wasn't long before the bell went. The playground and going home were the worst times. But French, which he thought would be okay, went badly. Mrs Taylor, a six-foot giant with masses of frizzy ginger hair and a temper to match, asked them to get in twos for conversation about La Normandie. A lot of them were going on a trip to Normandy at half-term. Unfortunately he didn't manage to get a partner. The numbers were odd. He looked for Louise and Rachel to make a three, but they weren't there. So he spent the whole lesson reading the textbook. Mrs Taylor didn't notice – she was marking books – till the end of the lesson when she collected in the work and he hadn't done it.

Then she said, 'Why haven't you done this?'

But before he could explain that he couldn't write down the conversation, because he hadn't had a partner to have a conversation with, she snapped, 'No excuses. Do it tonight or you'll have a detention.'

Then Nick said, 'He *is* new, Mrs Taylor,' as if he was the kindest child that ever lived.

Then it was RE which was utter chaos as usual because nobody saw the point of it. And because Mrs Vincent the teacher was fat and no one saw the point of her. Kev Walsh just wandered round the class saying he was looking for his bag. Mrs Vincent said she wanted them to discuss Jesus and pacifism, but as soon as she mentioned turning the other cheek, Kev mooned and the class collapsed with laughter. So she gave up and told them to copy a map of the Holy Land instead. Hardly anyone did that. Danny wanted to but couldn't find his pencil case. He thought Kev Walsh had hidden it, but during break he found it in Froggy Lewis's drawer. So he went down to the playground and told him.

He said, 'Why did you place my pencil case in your drawer?'

Lewis said, 'I didn't.' He grinned. Lewis always grinned. He was the smallest boy in the class, with the largest mouth. It stretched from ear to ear like a frog's.

Then he said, 'Wanna fight?' He had a squeaky voice.

Danny said, 'No, of course not.'

But during dinner break Lewis came up to him, as he came out of the boys' toilets and punched him in the chest.

Then he fell over.

Lewis punched Danny, then *Lewis* fell over!

Danny was trying to work out what had happened, when Big George who was just behind Lewis began a chant of 'Bull-y! Bull-y!'

Everybody it seemed took up the chant.

Then Kev punched Danny on the arm. And this time. because it hurt, or because of what his dad had said, Danny kicked out. At which point a teacher appeared and grabbed Danny by the shoulder.

'What's this?' he said.

'This new kid punched little Lewis,' said Big George, still helping Lewis to his feet. 'Kev went to help, then this new kid kicked Kev.'

The teacher looked from Danny to Lewis and said, 'Bullying will not be tolerated in this school – by anyone. Haven't you read the Code of Conduct?'

When he'd gone Kev said, 'We're going to beat you up, on Monday, Baa Lamb.'

That night Danny told his parents that he didn't think he was the right material for Lindley High either. He didn't want to go any more. He told them everything he could remember.

5

When Nick saw Danny's mother at school, first thing on Monday morning, he couldn't help feeling a flicker of apprehension. Mrs Lamb was coming out of the Head of Year's office at the end of the corridor. Danny, he'd just noted during register, wasn't at school. What had the prat said? What had his mummy said to Mrs Geary?

When Nick gave Mrs Geary a letter from his father, she didn't ask how his father was as she usually did. In fact she was rather abrupt.

Back in class he mentioned what he'd seen to Callum.

Callum said, 'It's probably about Friday. We didn't do nothing, did we?'

Word soon got round. During Geography Kevin, Lewis and Big George were sent for.

When the lesson ended without anyone else being sent for Nick relaxed a bit. He hadn't done anything. He had nothing to worry about. But when they didn't appear at morning break he started to worry again. Were they being given the third degree? What had Mrs Lamb said? What were they saying? They didn't appear at lunchtime either – in the dining room or the playground. Someone said they'd been given their lunch in the deputy's room. It was sometimes used for interrogations. Mr Scott, the deputy, believed in making people sweat.

Lewis and Big George eventually turned up in

afternoon register. Then they only had time to say that Kev had been suspended – before Mrs Pepper came in looking as if someone had died.

She took the register in her special sad voice. They knew by now to expect a lecture whenever she used it. The last one had been about bad behaviour on public transport. Then she hitched herself on the front of her table and said she was very, *very* sad and wanted to have a little chat with them. She asked them to bring their chairs to the front and arrange them in a half circle. She looked like a spaniel, Nick thought, with her mournful spaniel eyes and floppy spaniel hair.

'You'll all have noticed that Danny isn't here today,' she began, then paused blinking for maximum dramatic effect. It was obvious that she was going to try and make them all feel guilty. Well she wouldn't succeed as far as he was concerned. The prat deserved everything he got.

'Danny, I'm sorry to say, hasn't been happy at Lindley so far, and *some people* have been less than kind it seems. There was a nasty incident on Friday.' She said that Danny had been bullied in the playground and people had lied to Mr Spinks about what had really happened. Nick felt Callum nudge him as Mrs Pepper sucked in her bottom lip and looked round the circle of faces.

'I have to say I'm surprised by some of the names mentioned.' She paused again. 'Kevin, you'll note has been suspended for lying and bullying and other unacceptable behaviour over a period of time. *He* has been very unkind. Anyway,' she went on, suddenly brisk as she looked at the clock on the back wall, 'I'm sure no one else has been deliberately unkind, but I'd like you all to think about Danny. Think how you would feel if you were new – nervous perhaps, frightened even. And then start making amends, shall we? I, perhaps, haven't been as helpful as I could. But let's put the past behind us. When Danny comes back I want *all* of us to make a big effort to be very caring and supportive of him. Bullying will not be tolerated at Lindley, that shouldn't need saying. We have a Code of Conduct and Mrs Geary and I . . . '

Callum nudged Nick again and Nick put up his hand. 'Excuse me, Mrs Pepper, has Danny Lamb been suspended?'

'No, of course not. He's not well. Why should he?'

'Because on Friday *he* was bullying too.'

'Danny?'

'Yes,' said Nick. 'He started it. He punched Lewis, after accusing him of pinching his pencil case.'

'The smallest kid in the class,' said Callum.

'Did you take his pencil case, Lewis?'

'No, I didn't.'

'Well,' said Mrs Pepper, who couldn't remember all the details she'd just heard from Mrs Geary, 'there are usually two sides. But poor Danny obviously has something of a *friendship problem* and I think we must all do what we can to help him fit into our class. He finds the *playground experience* particularly painful, his mother says, and what Mrs Geary proposes is this.'

She went on to say that Danny was going to be given

permission to stay in at breaks with one other person.

Nick couldn't believe his ears.

'Who's that other person then?' laughed Callum. 'Me?'

'Whoever Danny chooses,' said the teacher. 'Each day he can ask one other person to go to the library or the computer room or the resources centre with him.'

'And must that person go?' Nick couldn't stop himself. He was incredulous.

'Yes, of course. It wouldn't be kind to refuse, would it? We want to empower Danny you see, give him some control over his own life.'

'But everyone else has to go outside whatever the weather?' said Callum.

'We all stay inside when it's raining, don't we?' Mrs Pepper smiled sweetly.

Nick was incensed. Why should this nerdish kid get this favoured treatment? What a load of namby-pamby crap! *Think about how nervous you were when you started Lindley. How frightened!* Well, *he* hadn't run home to his mummy when he'd been got at for talking posh, as the others called it, when he started Lindley. He'd told them straight that he spoke proper English and they didn't. He'd stuck up for himself. His anger grew throughout the afternoon. He was outraged that Mrs Pepper told them off when it was all Danny Lamb's fault. He didn't know how to act. Of course he had *a friendship problem.* He didn't have to wear his hair like that. He didn't have to say such prattish things. He didn't have to get his mummy into school to get them all into trouble and change the school rules just for him.

The only good thing about the day was that a lot of other people in the class agreed with him. That became obvious.

Later in Geography which she taught, Mrs Pepper said there was just one more thing. Did they know that Danny had eaten his lunch alone *every single day* since he'd been to Lindley. His mother had said so. Would they all, please, see that this didn't happen again?

6

Mrs Pepper felt that she had sorted things out. Her little talk to 7Y had gone well, and during the dinner hour she'd rung Mrs Lamb to suggest some things that might make things better for Danny when he returned. That he had his hair cut for instance, in a style to be more like the other boys. She'd also suggested that Danny come on the school trip to Normandy at half-term. Out of school activities always helped bonding and group cohesion, and it looked as if there was going to be a spare place as Kevin Walsh had been told he couldn't come. She hadn't been surprised to learn that he'd been one of the boys bullying Danny. The main one almost certainly. The others had indulged in some name-calling it seemed, but Mrs Lamb had probably exaggerated its extent. The mother was right to have mentioned it, of course. It was best to have these matters in the open. Everyone knew that bullying thrived on secrecy.

There were a couple more things to do – firstly see Mrs Geary about moving Toby Peters into 7Y. Mrs Lamb had said that Danny and Toby were close friends. Well, 7Y was a bit low on numbers compared to 7X. Numbers would be even lower if Kevin Walsh was permanently excluded as most of the staff hoped he would be. Secondly, she would also have a tactful word with Louise and Rachel. It seemed that they had been kind to Danny, mothered him in a way, but that might have actually *caused* some of the teasing. It would be better if Danny made friends with some of the boys.

When she got home Danny's mum assured him that she'd put matters right. She told him that Kevin Walsh was going to be suspended. She asked him if he would like to have his hair cut. When he said no she didn't press the point. His hair wasn't long, just longer than the current fashion. Well, Danny wasn't a follower of fashion. He was more positive about the French trip, because he had a real passion for languages, especially Latin, of course. He'd loved practising his French on family holidays. He said he thought he'd like to go to Normandy, especially when she said Toby was going and that he might be moved into the same class.

She'd discovered that there had been a problem with Toby, but managed to sort that out too. She'd got onto Gilly Peters straightaway and Gilly had soon got back to say Toby had not bullied Danny on the way home from school or at any other time. She'd talked to him about it. He hadn't been *with* the group who had persecuted him on the way home. He'd been behind them, for part of the way anyway, keeping an eye on Danny in fact. Danny had misinterpreted the situation.

The Peters were all coming to lunch a week on Sunday.

Danny didn't know what to think. He didn't feel reassured by his mother's assurances. He certainly didn't think having his hair cut would make any difference. On Tuesday morning he had a terrible headache. At breakfast his dad said, 'The sooner you face them the better, Danny.'

But his mum said he could have another day off if he really felt bad. He'd have to go back to bed and stay there though, and he couldn't watch television. Mrs Zielinsky, the help, would keep an eye on him. If his headache got worse Elsa would make an appointment for Danny to see the doctor. As soon as the house went quiet his headache vanished. Mrs Zielinsky brought him a cup of tea and a Kit-Kat then went downstairs and started vacuuming. He started to read a really interesting book about the Romans. Who needed school? He was perfectly capable of teaching himself.

But on Wednesday he had to go to school. His mum took him. She said she was sure he'd be okay now. Mrs Pepper had rung the previous evening to ask about Danny and to tell them that Kevin Walsh had been excluded indefinitely. She also said that Toby was going to be moved into 7Y.

When Mrs Geary told Toby that they'd like to move him into 7Y, it didn't occur to him to say no. He couldn't help feeling that it was promotion. He'd always felt that 7X was a lower stream. The best brains and even the best football players seemed to be in 7Y. Incredibly he'd forgotten all about Danny being there too, despite the fact that he'd heard nothing but Danny this, Danny that for days on end.

'Danny's not happy at Lindley, Elsa says.'

'Danny's not happy.'

Then had come the shocked interrogation. 'Toby, you haven't been bullying Danny?'

Fortunately he'd been able to explain to his mother what had really happened on the way home.

But as soon as he walked into the new class on Friday he realised he'd made a mistake. There he was with books and stuff piled up to his chin – and there was Danny at a desk with the only empty place in the room beside him – the only empty place. Toby checked as Danny beamed at him. The double desks were more or less in lines and all the others were occupied.

Mrs Irons, who was quite old – she had short white hair – pointed to the empty place.

'Oh yes, sit down there, Toby. You're transferring, aren't you?'

He was pleased in a way, that there was no choice. But he soon learned that he'd done the wrong thing.

Even though the desks were in lines, it was as if there was a ring round Danny, that no one crossed. Callum Nolan was holding his nose and leaning back as if overcome by fumes and Nick was laughing. So were a few others. Mrs Irons didn't notice. Danny didn't notice either. He just carried on beaming as Toby approached.

It was History. The class all had maps of Europe in front of them, two maps in fact and Mrs Irons brought Toby a set. She said that in Map A they were shading in areas where the Romans were in occupation. In Map B they were shading in areas where the Nazis had occupied Europe in the Second World War. There was a box of coloured pencils on her desk if he hadn't got any of his own. Fortunately Toby had a set of his own because the box on her desk was empty and people didn't seem eager to share the ones they had. They certainly weren't sharing with Danny who hadn't started. So Toby shared his with Danny.

Unfortunately, Mrs Pepper's talk to 7Y hadn't had the effect she intended. A lot of the class resented being made to feel guilty about Danny. Most people hadn't done anything bad to him. They didn't want to do anything bad to him, but they didn't want to spend their breaks with him either. Two boys, Simon Cartwright and Tim Dent had each spent one break with him in the computer room, but they'd declined next time he asked. The girls who would have been willing had been warned off. So when Mrs Pepper said that Toby Peters was joining the class to be a friend to Danny the overwhelming emotion was relief. It took the pressure off. Toby and Danny could get on with it as far as most people were concerned.

When the bell rang everyone left the room quickly, except Danny, of course.

'Stay with me, Toby,' he said. 'You can.'

But Toby said he felt like a breath of fresh air. He did. It was a nice day. The sun was shining. He hurried out with Danny in tow.

When they got to the playground he said, 'I'm going to play footie, okay? I always play footie.'

The game had started. He didn't want to be with Danny all the time, that was all. He'd told his mum that he'd be kind to Danny, but also that he didn't want to be his best friend any more, not like in the Infants. What was the point of their both being outcasts? Unfortunately Danny still couldn't take a hint. He stayed by Toby as he crossed the yard to where the game was taking place – and Toby couldn't get into it. Nobody passed him the ball. It was as if he was invisible while Danny was there. Danny said, 'They won't let me play either, but we could go to the resources centre.'

Toby said, 'I'm going to the bog. *Don't* come.'

The boys' bogs were back in school.

On the way in he met Callum Nolan coming out.

'You'll have to choose,' Callum said.

There was no mistaking what he meant.

The first lesson after break was French in the language lab. Toby tried to get there early, before Danny so that he could sit in a different place. It was important. He didn't mind sitting next to him *sometimes*. He just didn't want to sit next to him all the time. He wanted to have other friends in 7Y. But Mrs Fairweather, his 7X teacher, waylaid him, so when he reached the lab it was action replay of the first time, except that Danny was sitting near the door this time, with the one empty place beside him. He was reading.

The teacher hadn't arrived yet.

Toby could feel people looking at him.

They were watching to see what he would do.

Toby glanced at what Danny was reading. It was his *Teach Yourself Latin* book.

PUER n. boy

PUER v.

PUER acc.
PUERIS gen.

And he suddenly remembered Danny telling him that PUER was Latin for boy, and he remembered him laughing about it. *Danny had made a joke about it!*

Toby held up the book.

'Listen to this,' he said. 'Do you know what the Latin for boy is? PU-ER!' He sounded it out, pointing to the words.

Someone laughed.

'Danny told me.' That seemed to get lost.

Toby hoped Danny was laughing too.

'Let me look.' Nick Tate appeared from somewhere. He took the book from Toby and said, 'Nice one, Tobe. We all knew Danielle here smelled. Now we know why. It's all the Latin he does. Swot here's a POO-ER!'

He held his nose.

Then he raised his arms and began to conduct the class in a loud whispered chant, bringing in first one side, then the other. Almost everyone joined in.

'Dani-elle, do you smell?'

'Yes, you do. You're a poo!

Let's all flush him down the loo!'

Toby looked down at Danny, willing him to laugh. It was *his* joke. But he was just gazing at Toby, calf-eyes wide open.

Someone lobbed a rubber at him.

He should have lobbed it back.

Then someone said Mrs Taylor was coming.

Instantly they all returned to their places.

'*Bonjour mes élèves!*'

'*Bon-jour Ma-dame!*' they droned.

Everybody sat down.

Toby sat by Danny. He did. Then Mrs Taylor asked them to get into twos for *conversation* and Nick asked Toby to be his partner.

7

As they made their way to the back of the lab Nick said, 'Is he a friend of yours?'

Toby said, 'Our families are friends. It's difficult.'

He knew he'd hurt Danny though he hadn't meant to. He hadn't. The joke had backfired or side-fired, gone all wrong anyway. Or half-wrong. If only Danny had laughed. It had been his joke first.

He wanted to say, 'Leave him alone. Just leave him alone.' But the words didn't come out.

Besides, Danny was alone. He was sitting alone at the desk by the door. There were still twenty-seven in the class – Kev had gone but Toby had joined – so there would always be an odd one and there was no question who that would be.

Mrs Taylor said, 'For heaven's sake, boy, make a three.'

Simon Cartwright and Tim Denton asked Danny to join them.

In *conversation* – which was supposed to be about buying a meal in *La Normandie* and in French – Nick told Toby about Mrs Pepper's *lecture*. About how she'd said they'd all got to be *très gentil* to Danny, and about how she'd changed the school *règles* just for him. He explained how Danny could stay inside at breaks and lunchtimes and how he could choose any one of them to stay inside with him.

'So,' said Nick, 'if you don't want to be Danny's best *ami* you'd better make sure you're not asked.'

When the bell went Toby got out sharp before Danny could speak to him. Nick and Callum were close behind. They seemed to want him as their friend. The three of them went to look at the fixtures board, then into the dinner hall, where Danny was sitting on his own till Louise and Rachel joined him.

Nick noticed him noticing and said, 'See, he's all right. Not your responsibility.'

Callum said, 'As I said, you've got to choose.'

After dinner Nick picked Toby first for his playground team. He said he thought Toby was good enough for the first team.

When they went back in for afternoon school the three of them went in together and sat down together near the front.

As Louise came in she stopped at their table and said, 'You're a right Judas, you are.' Danny must have told her about their being friends once.

Nick told him not to worry about it.

Danny and Rachel came in a few minutes later. Danny was telling her that the word oval came from *ovum*, the Latin for egg. The plural was *ova* and ovaries were where eggs were made.

Danny walked home alone that night, as usual. He didn't mind. At least no one was following him or 'keeping an eye on him'. He didn't want anyone's eye on him. His mum had been completely wrong about Toby. So his day hadn't been as good as he'd hoped. But it hadn't been as bad as he feared either. Toby's betrayal had been the worst bit. But Tim and Simon had been kind in French. They told him not to take any notice of Nick. Tim said he was a nasty piece of work, but unfortunately none of the teachers realised. Louise and Rachel had been kind to him too. He'd told them how upset he was. He'd told them how Toby used to be his best friend, and they'd been very understanding. He'd felt devastated in French when Toby made fun of him. It had been hard not to cry. He'd tried telling himself that Toby hadn't meant it. But his actions afterwards made clear he had. Toby hadn't said one word to him all afternoon, even though they were in the same class. He was friends with Nick and Callum now. Toby had joined the other side.

When he got home Toby's mum was in the kitchen, having a cup of tea with his mum. They were looking at a map of France. His mum said they were talking about the school trip.

Gilly Peters said, 'Hi, Danny! How are you? Let me show you where you're going.'

But he went straight upstairs to his room. How could he tell them what had happened? His mum seemed so sure she'd put everything right. Perhaps they'd both see the real situation when all the Peters came to lunch.

The next week at school wasn't too bad, though only Louise or Rachel would stay in with him at lunchtimes. Sometimes he stayed in on his own. He usually stayed in the library and got on with his homework. But on Friday lunchtime when everyone stayed in because it was raining, he couldn't get on with his technology homework because he couldn't find his technology project. It had been in his drawer in the morning.

When he told Mrs Pepper during register she said, 'We mustn't jump to conclusions, must we, Dan?'

Then she said, 'You *are* okay now?' And he said yes, because she seemed to want him to. But Toby hadn't said a word to him since last Friday, and he might have to start his technology project all over again.

Before they went off to lessons Mrs Pepper asked everybody to keep a lookout for Danny's project.

Danny wished Toby wasn't coming on Sunday. How would he act? What had he told his parents?

Toby hadn't told them anything. He planned to do exactly as he always had done when they went round to the Lambs for lunch. He'd be polite and friendly to everyone including Danny. But at school he'd keep out of his way as much as possible. He had no choice but to live a double life.

Sunday arrived and it helped that the grown-ups behaved as they had done for years. The Lambs ate in their Victorian dining room on Sundays. They'd restored the room to exactly how it would have looked in Victorian times, they said, with flowery wallpaper and heavy velvet curtains. The antique furniture was heavy and dark, and the two families sat at an enormous round table laid with a white tablecloth. The only thing lacking was servants. So Danny's dad carved the leg of lamb and you had to help yourself to vegetables from fancy tureens. The grown-ups drank red wine and their voices got louder and louder. Toby heard his dad telling Danny's dad that he now had sixty people under him at Glossop's where he worked. Then Danny's dad said his department was doubling in size. The mothers talked about books and Polly and Jess giggled a lot. They were both wearing velvet dresses with lace collars, and they were trying to be seen and not heard like real Victorian children. Nobody seemed to notice that Toby and Danny were much quieter than usual. They were sitting next to each other and Toby couldn't think of anything to say, though he wanted to.

Danny didn't want to. He wanted to go to his own room and stay there.

After lunch Danny's dad said, 'Museum, lads?' – as he had so many times before. Then he drove them into the centre of Allton as it was raining again. He left them at the entrance to the museum which was next to the Town Hall, saying Toby's dad would pick them up at tea-time.

Hoping they wouldn't meet anyone from school, Toby led the way in. He thought about saying sorry for the 'puer' incident, and explaining how it had been a mistake, but decided against it. Danny would definitely forgive him and then expect to be his best friend again. And he didn't want to be Danny's best friend. In fact he didn't want Danny as any sort of friend. That was the truth of it. He had lots of friends he preferred now and Danny got in the way and made him feel uncomfortable. He'd grown out of Danny. Why did that cause so much trouble?

To be friendly – but not too friendly – he said, 'Let's look at the Roman stuff, shall we?'

The Romans were Danny's favourite.

To start with they looked at a lot of statues without arms and Danny studied the notice by each one. Then they looked at some Roman coins and a letter, in Latin of course, from a Roman soldier to his mum. Danny got really excited about this, though he'd seen it umpteen times before. It began '*O me miserum*' which meant *Woe is me!* he said. The soldier was up north guarding Hadrian's Wall and he was very fed up. He was asking his mum to send him clean socks and underpants. Danny explained that *miles* was Latin for soldier and gave us the word 'military'. *Miserum* gave us 'misery' and so on. And so on.

Toby let him burble on because it was quite interesting and because they had to fill the time somehow. Danny burbled on because he couldn't bear the muddle in his head when he was silent.

Was Toby his friend or wasn't he? He seemed friendly at the moment. He hadn't said sorry though. Had he really been so cruel and horrible? Now it seemed hard to believe.

Suddenly, nice as anything, Toby said, 'Let's look at the picture, shall we?'

Danny knew which one he meant and followed him to the gallery upstairs. It was a hunting scene, full of action and bright colours. When they were little they'd decided that it was their favourite thing in the whole museum, or at least their favourite picture. It stood out because the others in the room were old and dark and mostly of the crucifixion. They hated those. Their picture was old too, but was full of *life*. The men on horseback wore red and yellow, and fired arrows as they raced along. They *rained* arrows. It was a really exciting picture.

But today, when he stood before it, Danny didn't like it at all. He couldn't see what he ever had liked about it. All he could see was a deer with arrows in its side.

Toby said, 'It's great, isn't it?'

Danny had the head-in-a-muddle feeling again. Poor deer. Everything had changed. Nothing was nice any more.

On the way home Toby told his own dad that they'd had a good time. Danny stared out of the window. When they got home all the grown-ups agreed that it had been a really nice get-together. They said they must do it again soon.

And Toby said, 'See you,' as he left.

But at school the next day he behaved as if Danny was invisible. He didn't even look at him.

On Wednesday night there was a meeting at school about the French trip. Danny wasn't sure now that he wanted to go, but his mum said it would be good for him. Louise and Rachel said it would be great. He and his mum arrived in the dining hall at the same time as Toby and his, and the two mothers immediately sat down beside each other on the front row, the boys beside them. Toby said, 'Hi,' but that was all. Soon Nick Tate arrived with his mother and father. His father, who was wearing his uniform, wandered off towards the staff-room while the mothers all greeted each other like friends, and behaved as if the three boys were friends too. Nick sat down beside Toby.

Danny read the programme of events on the blackboard in front of them.

CALVADOS/Normandy

1. **Departure time from Lindley High, Monday 26th October 3.45 am. (Arrive and park on playground 3.20 am)**
2. **Arrive back at Lindley High Sunday 1st November 8.30 pm.**
3. **E111 form into school by Friday 16th October.**
4. **Pocket money maximum of £35 for spending in France. If you require this to be changed into Francs by school, money to be in by Friday 16th October.**

He heard his mum offering to get French money for all of them, if they hadn't got it, because the deadline for the school getting it was well past. His mum worked part-time at the bank.

5. **All medication including inhalers to be handed to Mrs Irons on arrival at school.**

Then he couldn't read any more because Callum and his mum arrived and stood in front of the blackboard. Callum's eyes looked a bit red and Mrs Nolan looked cross. Mrs Tate called her over. There was a problem it seemed. Mrs Nolan had to go away on Sunday night and Callum's father couldn't help. He'd gone back to Scotland. Danny heard Mrs Tate saying that Callum could stay with Nick. She'd see that both boys got to the coach on time. Then Mrs Taylor and Mrs Irons and Mr O'Kelly the PE teacher came in and the official meeting began.

Mrs Taylor said she and Mrs Irons and Mr O'Kelly were the teachers accompanying the group to the study centre at Brion sur Mer in Calvados, Normandy. Mrs Bridges, the school secretary would also be going – and her husband. Parents could feel confident that their children would be very well looked after, but the young people would, of course, have to behave impeccably themselves. For that reason only completely reliable children had been allowed on the trip. She said that many educational outings had been arranged – to see the Bayeux Tapestry and several of the Normandy landing sites. The latter was relevant to the National Curriculum, as all Year 7 pupils were studying the Second World War in history. There would also be lots of team games, organised by Mr O'Kelly the PE teacher. However, the young people would also be allowed to go off in small groups on occasions, to practise their French by going to shops and cafés on their own. There would, of course, always be an adult in the vicinity.

Danny carried on reading the programme of events.

Toby watched the parents who were all listening avidly. Some asked questions. Mr Tate, who stood at the side, asked about insurance cover and the route. He asked why they were going via Calais when Cherbourg would have been more sensible. Toby thought he was being a bit embarrassing but Nick didn't seem to mind. Someone else asked about seat-belts on the coach.

Then they all had to collect folders full of leaflets from a table at the side. While this went on Toby heard Danny's mum tell his mum that he could stay with Danny on Sunday night. That way only one of them would have to get up at an unearthly hour. Toby's mum said thanks very much, and that she would collect a week later. Nick, who was standing near Toby, nudged him and looked sympathetic. Toby was pleased in a way that Nick could see what the situation was. It was difficult but there was nothing he could do about it. He shook his head when Nick leaned over and muttered, 'Don't worry, I'll think of something.'

There was nothing anyone could do.

Nick had other ideas.

He couldn't stand Danny now. It was hard to explain – and he didn't try – but the mere sight of him made him feel as if something inside him was going to explode. He didn't want Danny to come on the French trip. It would spoil it, like it had spoiled Lindley High. Before Danny came everything had been all right. When he got home he wrote a letter, on his word processor.

Dear Mrs Lamb,
We think you ought to know that your Danny is not as perfect as you think he is. The reason we don't

like him is that he's quite mean sometimes. He kicked Lewis and he broke Toby's Walkman. That's why nobody wants to be his friend.

So please don't keep asking us to like him. It would be better if he didn't come on the trip. He wouldn't enjoy it.

From Toby and Lewis's friends.

He posted it next day, so that it would arrive on Friday or Saturday at the latest. In time anyway for Mrs Lamb to decide not to send her wet son on the French trip.

But on Monday morning at 3.35 am, in the middle of the night, a bleary-eyed Nick, sitting on the back seat of the coach with Callum, Froggy Lewis and Big George, saw Danny arrive. He could hardly believe it as he saw Danny's mother's yellow 2CV, and then Danny and Toby getting out of it. Mrs Lamb had brought them both as she had planned. As the two boys climbed onto the coach Nick called for Toby to join them. Toby, who had been listening to Danny talking about the French Resistance for the last three hours, went to the back thankfully.

Louise and Rachel were sitting just inside the door. They told Danny to sit down opposite them on the seat they'd saved for him. Danny was pleased. He was tired. If he had a seat to himself he could lie down. The coach was a fifty-seater and there were only forty pupils on the trip. Even counting the teachers, there was plenty of room. Some people were lying down already. He told the girls he'd had a nice evening with Toby. They'd played Monopoly with Jess and his dad, till about eleven when his mum made them go to bed to get some sleep. But then they'd talked. He had a good book about the French Resistance and Toby had been interested in hearing all about it. He thought they were friends again and the holiday would be okay.

8

Nick was furious that Danny had appeared. He stood up so Toby could get into the corner seat on the back row.

'Didn't she get it?'

Toby didn't know what Nick was talking about. Nick assumed he'd know all about the letter by now. Now he had to explain – keeping his voice low.

'But he didn't...' Toby sensed Nick's exasperation and didn't finish. The lights were dim at the back of the coach, so he couldn't see his face clearly.

'He punched Kev, didn't he?'

'Because Kev...'

'Sorry, I forgot you were his friend.' Nick made as if he was going to stand up again. 'You can go and sit with him if you like... Ginger.'

Callum leant across and ruffled Toby's hair. 'Go on, Ginger. Sit with poo-boy.'

Then Mrs Taylor who was near the front, stood and called for quiet. She introduced Ted the driver who was an oldish man with a pony tail, and said she hoped they'd all be very considerate and not make too much noise. Then she began to call a register.

Outside in the darkness one or two cars were driving off, but most parents were waiting for the bus to leave before they went home. Toby was sure Elsa Lamb was out there somewhere, watching anxiously, and part of him wanted to rush out and explain the letter that she'd soon receive, and deny everything in it. If he didn't, and even if he did, there was going to be a lot of explaining to do when he got home – if the mothers waited that long. He could see the scene now – Elsa, hysterical, ringing his mum, his mum being super reasonable saying, 'Let's not jump to conclusions. Let's ask the boys. Let's ask Tobe. We can telephone France.'

This was going to ruin the holiday. Nick hadn't thought it through.

'C-Callum Nolan!' Mrs Taylor's microphone crackled.

'Yes, Mrs Taylor!'

'Toby Peters!'

'Yes.'

'Toby? Are you here? Speak up will you!'

'Yes, Mrs Taylor!'

Callum said, 'You'll look daft if you deny it. We'll all say it's true. We saw him kick you as well, didn't we?'

'We' was Callum, Big George and Lewis. Toby could see them now, all on the back seat. Froggy Lewis, grinning in the opposite corner said, 'Yup. Then we saw him break your Walkman.'

'But it isn't broken.' It was in the bag at his feet. Toby felt sick.

'That's easily sorted,' said Big George and the others laughed.

Maybe the letter wouldn't arrive. Maybe it had got lost. That's why it hadn't arrived. Maybe Nick hadn't really done this. Toby tried to think of something that would make himself feel better and failed.

'Nick Tate!'

'Mais oui, Madame Taylor!' Nick slung his arm round Toby's shoulders as he spoke. 'I did it for *you*, Tobe, to save you spending all your time being mummy to little poo-boy. It'll be fine, you'll see. We'll stick together, like ... ' He turned to include the others. '... the *five* musketeers! That's us! All for one and one for all!'

He raised his arm in a salute and the others followed, as the lights flickered and the engine roared into action.

Some of the girls shouted, ''Bye!' and waved towards the darkness outside. Then the bus pulled out into the drive, lighting up the waiting cars. As it swung round, Toby glimpsed Elsa Lamb, standing by her little yellow car waving frantically. From his seat at the front Danny waved back to her.

Then the bus stopped again at the top of the drive and Mrs Taylor stood and picked up the microphone again. 'Listen, everyone, I think it would be a good idea if we all tried to get some sleep now. It's a three-hour drive to Dover where we're aiming to catch the 8 o'clock ferry. Most of you have got reclining seats, so make yourselves as comfortable as you can. In a few minutes we'll dim the lights.'

In the darkness with warm air blowing from a heater nearby, Danny fell asleep quite soon. Toby wished he could stretch out but there wasn't a lot of room on the back seat. Besides Big George produced a pack of cards and said, 'Who's for a game of Black Jack?' The game took his mind off the letter for some of the time at least.

Nick said he didn't want to play and swapped seats with Toby. He needed time to think – and calm down. The window by his face steamed up as thinking about Danny made his breath come faster. The prat had better keep out of Toby's way and not make a nuisance of himself, expecting to be his best friend, his partner like in the Infants. Fortunately stupid Mrs Pepper wasn't with them, watching to see they were all being *caring* to dear little Danny. Caring was what had made him into a namby-pamby prat. His daft mother was caring. Now, what would she do when she got the letter? Nick thought it out logically.

1. Mrs Lamb would worry about her little lambkin, Danny – that he'd gone away for a whole week and might not be having a nice time. He *wouldn't* be having a nice time!

2. She'd want to go running up to school to complain, but wouldn't be able to as school was closed for half-term. And if she went when they got back, she'd just learn that her darling boy wasn't perfect – that he deserved what he got – because Big George, Callum, Lewis and Toby would all swear that he had punched Lewis. He *had* kicked Kev, so it was *perfectly fair* that they gave him some of his own medicine. It would do him good.

3. She might ring the emergency number that all parents had been given and ask to speak to a teacher. Yes, she would think this was an emergency. But she wouldn't know who to complain about. That's why he hadn't signed it. Teachers hated fuss-pot parents, anyway.

Nick thought it out carefully, step by step. He must take care not to be seen being less than nice to the prat. Someone might have to see to Toby's Walkman. He must make sure no bad reports got back to his own parents. *They* weren't soft like Danny's. Nick doodled a row of SSs in the steamed-up window as the words softly softly came into his head. He mustn't do anything to Danny that he could be blamed for. Even if it was good for him. In fact if the prat had the sense to keep out of their way, it might be better just to ignore him, like his dad had ignored him once, for a whole week, when he'd done something to annoy him. That hurt. Yes, that would probably be best.

Danny did keep out of their way for the journey to Dover anyway, which took longer than expected for some reason. He slept for most of the journey, and didn't wake up till people started shouting as they arrived at the ferry port and saw the sea for the first time. Then he saw the sea, and the white cliffs of Dover towering round them, and the seagulls wheeling overhead in a clear blue sky, and he started to feel excited too. Unfortunately there was a delay at the port, and they had to spend over an hour in the coachpark waiting for some lorry drivers to move off. But the weather was sunny and Mrs Taylor said they could get out and explore, as long as they kept the coach in view. Most people got off, but he stayed on the coach – on his seat near the front – watching the vehicles rolling on and off the ferry boats. The driver stayed too and closed the door when Danny said he didn't like the smell of diesel coming in from outside. Danny was delighted when he saw the name of the ferry they were going on, because it had a Latin name, *Invicta*, which meant unvanquished! It was a huge white modern boat, and when Louise and Rachel reappeared – they'd gone off to find some loos – he told them he felt joyful and hopeful about its name and they were really nice to him. Later, as he stood on deck with them, watching the white cliffs of Dover getting further and further away, he felt as if he was leaving all his troubles behind him. And when the coach rolled onto French soil at last, he joined in with everyone's cheers.

He was glad he'd brought a good book with him though, because the first bit of the journey in France was slow and boring. They were on the N1, because the motorway was still being built, and there was a fifty kilometre per hour limit on most of it. At first the people who had never been to France before got excited when they saw a word they recognised on an advert, or a house with shutters or a set of French traffic lights so dim you could hardly see them. But after about an hour of travelling along straight, tree-lined roads with flat fields on either side, tiredness and boredom set in. By the time the countryside got more interesting it was getting dark. To pass the time most people played cards or games like noughts and crosses or hangman, but he didn't mind that. He really enjoyed his book about the French Resistance.

Toby quite enjoyed the journey. It was a good feeling, being part of a gang. Nick was friendly and generous. When Toby discovered that Elsa had given him peanut butter sandwiches which he hated, Nick shared his packed lunch with him. So did the others, even Callum who wasn't the friendliest of types. Lewis and George were a good laugh. He couldn't help thinking about the letter from time to time, but he couldn't believe that Nick would do anything really bad to Danny. He just wasn't the sort. So there wasn't a lot to worry about it. If his mum rang he'd tell her that Danny was all right. He was. Some of the girls were looking after him.

When the sea came into view again after about three hours, there were more cheers, but by the time they arrived at Brion sur Mer everyone was tired and fed up with travelling. It was too dark to see much. A few twinkling lights showed where the sea was but they couldn't see much of the town. There weren't many lights and there was no one about to ask where the study centre was. Ted, the driver, parked the coach in the square where there was a Plan de Ville and fortunately it showed that the study centre was only a couple of roads away. It only took a few minutes to get there.

Unfortunately the tall gates were locked. Beyond them a solid looking building with pointed turrets loomed into the darkness. Their notes said it was an eighteenth-century château, which had been occupied by Nazis in the war, but by this time no one was interested in architecture or history. While Ted and Mrs Taylor went off to try and find someone to open the main gates, people started to get their things together and joked about what the letters UNCMT on the gates stood for. Colditz, camp and concentration were favourites for the C. They were all looking forward to a decent meal and some freedom after being cramped up for so long. Toby, noticing Danny at the front, hoped he'd have the sense to keep a low profile.

Danny didn't, of course. It wasn't long before he was making a complete ass of himself. The decent meal didn't happen – that was the start of the trouble. They were welcomed, once they got inside, by Madame Bleu who wore a blue suit and had bluish hair scraped into a tight chignon. She told them to leave their bags and cases in the panelled entrance hall and go straight to the dining room where *le diner* was ready. Even before they sat down on benches – at a long table beneath a row of shields – they could smell something disgusting. The table was set with plates, soup bowls and cutlery and four enormous white tureens.

'*Potage au chou-fleur*,' Madame explained, lifting one of the lids.

'Cauliflower soup,' Mrs Taylor said, as if she thought the translation might make the slimy green stuff more attractive.

The staff and one or two pupils had a little. Most people started on the baguettes and hoped for better from the main course. Danny had two helpings. A nudge from Nick drew Toby's attention to this. Soon everyone knew because they had to wait for him to finish. He didn't even notice they were waiting for him. The second course looked more promising. Everyone felt better when they saw Madame Bleu and the chef passing mounds of frites and big dishes of sliced meat

66

through a serving hatch. The meat looked juicy and tender and smelled good. Someone had a taste and pronounced it edible, and the ancient, wood-panelled hall went quiet as everyone tucked in.

Then one of the girls said, '*Langue de boeuf*, Mrs Taylor. Doesn't that mean tongue of beef?' She was reading from a menu that she'd just noticed on the table. Word travelled quickly and most people stopped eating the meat. A few people made retching sounds till Mrs Taylor got to her feet and shouted at them. Then Madame Bleu appeared and the chef came out of the kitchen. They soon noticed all the uneaten food.

Madame Bleu started firing questions at everybody – in French – which nobody answered, except Mrs Taylor who said something about them all being too *fatigués* to eat. But then the chef spotted Danny's plate which looked as if he'd licked it clean. In fact, French style, he was wiping it with a chunk of baguette.

The chef nearly kissed him, and when he rattled away in French, Danny replied, saying something about *la sauce délicieuse*!

'*Comment t'appelles-tu?*' said the chef.

It was like a French lesson.

'*Je m'appelle Danny.*'

'*Regardez! Regardez Danny le gourmet.*' The chef went a bit mad waving his arms and spitting French at everyone.

Madame Bleu beamed at Danny. An English boy who liked *la cuisine française*! And who spoke French so well! She congratulated Mrs Taylor on her star pupil.

Danny beamed. He looked happy but all the praise did him no good at all.

Nobody, except Danny, ate the hard little pears they served for dessert.

After dinner they headed down the corridor for the activities room at Mrs Taylor's request. Several people asked if they could go out and buy some decent food. A plan of the town on the back wall showed where the shops were, but the teacher said it was too late. Beside the plan was a list that showed them all which dorms they'd been allocated to, and a plan of the building. Mrs Taylor told them to consult the list and plan, then collect their luggage from the hall and make their way upstairs.

Danny was late coming out of the dining room, and it took him a while to find the activities room. When he arrived there was a crowd round the noticeboard. Shrieks of 'Good, we're together' and 'You're with us!' showed that most of the girls were happy with the dorm arrangements. Danny was keen to know who he was in with, but thought he'd wait till the rush was over. Hoping he was with Toby – and that he wasn't with Nick Tate's gang – he went to study a map of the Normandy coast on the opposite wall. He'd just found Brion sur Mer on Sword Beach, when the whining voice of Froggy Lewis penetrated his thoughts.

'Why does he have to be with us?'

Danny turned and there was Lewis flanked by Big George and Callum, complaining to Mrs Irons.

She said, 'No arguing, Lewis. That's what it says and

that's how it stays. Now get yourself and your luggage upstairs.'

Through the open door, Danny could see a very wide and grand staircase. which went in two different directions at the top. Some people were already lugging their bags up it, girls going one way, boys the other when they reached the top. Nick and Toby were standing at the bottom, beneath a carved eagle which crowned the newel post. Were they friends now? Danny hoped not, but they were standing side by side. Nick's lips were moving slightly, but they didn't seem to be talking to one another.

Nick and Toby were waiting for Lewis, Callum and George to return. Nick had sent the deputation to Mrs Irons. He was seething, and had been since he'd seen the list. Toby was a bit surprised to see him so worked up. Nick, usually so cool, was mumbling to himself. 'Prat. Prat. Prat. Prat. Namby-pamby *scum* prat. He is *not not not* going to be with us.'

When the crowd cleared Danny went to look at the list.

Chambre 7
Nick Tate
George McKay
Callum Nolan
Lewis Barnes
Toby Peters
Daniel Lamb

It made him feel nervous, but at least he was with Toby.

9

By the time Danny had picked up his bags and consulted the plan to find where Chambre 7 was, the others were all upstairs, on the other side of the doors at the top. The staff were still downstairs in a small staffroom, next to the activities room. He could see them through a half-open door, drinking coffee. Mrs Taylor had her feet up on the table.

He lugged his things upstairs and got a bit of a surprise. He thought the grand staircase would lead to something similar upstairs – tapestry hangings and four poster beds perhaps – but when he elbowed open the door at the top, he stepped into a long, musty-smelling corridor with grey vinyl on the floor and peeling yellow paint on the walls. Some doors had numbers on them but by no means all. Dull unvarnished patches showed where numbers had been, but there was no number 7. When he tried the door where 7 should logically have been, he found himself in a washroom with a row of basins on one side, showers on the other. Clearly that was where the smell was coming from. When he tried the next door that too seemed locked. Voices came from some of the rooms and he knocked on one of them but the boy who answered said the room was full.

In the end he went downstairs to consult the plan again, and Mrs Taylor saw him as he passed the staffroom door. She came out with a glass of wine in her hand.

'Danny! My star pupil – eh! What are you doing here?' She was just coming to check that everyone was in bed, she said.

He told her about not being able to find his room, and after a glance at the plan, she told him to follow her upstairs. He was surprised that she was so nice.

As she strode along the corridor she counted in French.

'*Un! Deux! Trois! Quatre! Cinq! Six!* And this should be it – *sept!*' she said triumphantly as she opened a door that had seemed locked when he'd tried it earlier.

A wedge of light from the corridor lit up two sets of bunk-beds at right angles to one another. Putting her head round the door, Mrs Taylor whispered that there was another set of bunks behind it, and that the bottom one was empty.

'Now get into bed as quickly as you can and try not to wake the others. They must be tired out,' she said. 'And don't forget to close the door when you're ready.'

He heard her footsteps getting fainter and fainter as he got his pyjamas out of his bag. Now he could see Callum Nolan on the top bunk, his pale face with its close-together eyes turned towards the door. He got undressed as quietly as he could. The room was warm thank goodness. He could hear water flowing through the central heating pipes. After he'd closed the door, he had to feel his way into his bunk, but it was a good feeling when his head hit the pillow and he snuggled under the duvet.

Then a voice from the darkness said, 'You can stay here tonight, Baa Lamb, but you'd better make other arrangements tomorrow.'

He slept through the alarm in the morning, and when he woke up the others weren't there. They'd gone down but they hadn't made their beds, he noticed, and there were pyjamas and crisp packets all over the floor. The sun was streaming in through the window. He got dressed quickly, put his pyjamas under his pillow and found a piece of paper there – with a game of hangman on it.

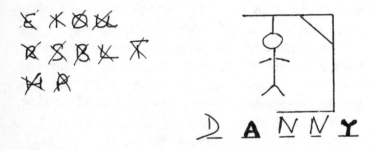

The man was hanging from the gibbet and there was a word underneath. D-A-N-N-Y. He couldn't see a wastebin so he put it in his pocket. Then he went to find the toilets.

Toby was in the corridor when he came out. Danny smiled but Toby didn't smile back.

He said, 'I've come to take you to breakfast, and remind you to make other arrangements.'

Mrs Taylor had sent him when she noticed Danny was missing. Mr O'Kelly had told her last night about the

72

two boys being friends. He said Mrs Pepper had told him so when he'd been drawing up the dorm lists.

Nick had told Toby to remind Danny about making other arrangements and thinking Danny mightn't have understood the phrase 'make other arrangements' he said, 'Ask to be put in another room. Say you're allergic to Callum's hair gel or something.'

Danny was allergic – to wasp stings. He always carried an antidote in case he got one, but Toby's remark didn't make sense. He followed Toby downstairs wondering what he meant. When they reached the dining room Toby pointed to an empty place at the end of the table near the door, then he went and sat by Nick.

Most people had finished eating. Some were pocketing the little packets of jam and sugar in case of starvation later. Danny helped himself to baguette and apricot jam. Louise brought him a big cup of hot chocolate.

She said, 'Bad luck about the room allocation. Were you okay?'

He said he was a bit nervous. She smiled and said, 'Nervous seems to be your favourite word. Cheer up.'

Then Mrs Taylor started telling them about arrangements for the day. First, she said, Mr O'Kelly would do a dorm inspection and award points. There was a prize at the end of the holiday for the tidiest dorm. After dorm inspection they were all going to explore Brion sur Mer. They had to pick up a worksheet from the table by the front door. It was a sort of quiz, and filling it in would help them find their way round and get to know their bearings. They could go in groups of four. It should take

73

them about an hour, and they were all to meet in the square by the library, *la bibliothèque* she reminded them, at 11 o'clock. Then, weather willing, they'd all have a game of rounders on the beach before lunch.

'After lunch...'

But Danny couldn't take in any more. Fortunately Louise said he could make up a four with Rachel and her and a girl called Patsy.

He waited for them in the hall as he had already tidied his bed. Through the open door he could see the garden. It wasn't a bit like an English garden. There weren't any flowers or grass, just a lot of gravel and some bushes carved into geometrical shapes. There had been a bit of frost and a line of them sparkled in the sunlight. He was just thinking how few birds there were in France when one landed near a triangular bush. It was a blackbird he thought, though there was a bit of white on one of its wings. It hopped about a bit and started pecking at something in the gravel when two more birds appeared. Then the new arrivals started flying at the first bird, pecking at it with their orange beaks – they *were* all blackbirds – trying to drive it away. The poor thing hopped under the bush but even then the others didn't stop. They chased it out the other side. Then more of them flew in and the flock of them started mobbing the white-winged bird. It was horrible and he covered his eyes with his hands, but he could still see them through the spaces between his fingers, and hear them, twittering and screeching as they attacked again and again, stabbing at the white-winged bird with their orange beaks.

Fortunately the girls appeared and when they saw what was happening, Patsy rushed out, waving her arms and the birds all flew off.

Afterwards she said, 'Why didn't you do something?'

And he didn't answer because he didn't know why.

Why? He kept thinking about it, till Louise told him to forget it and help with the questions. They had just walked out of the gates, turned left, crossed the square at the bottom of the narrow road, and found themselves looking at the sea. He felt calmer just looking at it. It was so calm and grey and seemed to enfold the little town of Brion sur Mer. *La mer*. Sea. *La mère*. Mother. He thought it was really interesting that the two French words sounded the same and said so to Rachel. She thought it was interesting too.

The sun was warm on their backs and it felt like a summer holiday, not an autumn one. The sky was a vast blue dome overhead, and there were palm trees in the gardens along the sea-front. The hotels and houses all looked closed though and the beach was deserted. They were the only people on it. As they walked along the sand Danny spotted a house covered with sea-shells which was the answer to one of the questions. Later, on their way to the town centre, he spotted some ceramic snails on a roof – which was the answer to another one. The girls were really pleased with him. They finished the quiz in record time, and spent the rest of the time buying postcards and stocking up on sweets. Then they went to look for a café.

*

Nick and Toby caught sight of them in the Café Domino.

The five musketeers were only four as Nick's request for them to be a five was turned down by Mrs Taylor. So Lewis had been sent to join another group.

'You did tell prat to make other arrangements, didn't you?' Nick asked Toby, when he saw Danny through the café window. He was writing a postcard – to his mummy probably. Louise was next to him, their heads close together. What a waste. Louise was the best looking girl in the class.

'Yes, but I'm not sure that he understood.'

'He'd better have.'

'He can ask to move in with the girlies,' said Callum.

Nick said he was sure the girls would prefer someone more spunky, himself for instance.

Big George laughed. Toby felt a bit uncomfortable, but after the game of rounders he felt better. Just running made him feel good and Danny was clearly okay. Mr O'Kelly said those who wanted to go for a walk along the beach could, and Danny had gone with Mr and Mrs Bridges who were the sort of middle-aged people he got on well with. Toby hoped he was telling them that he wanted to move to a different dorm. But Danny was telling Mrs Bridges about the snails. The day was going well as far as he was concerned.

In the afternoon they all caught a local bus along the coast road. It was Ted the driver's day off driving, but he came too and Mrs Irons pointed out famous landmarks, like the remains of the Mulberry Harbour at Arromanches. She said the Mulberry Harbour was the artificial harbour which the Allies had started dragging into place the night before D-day – June 6th 1944 – so they could surprise the Nazis by landing on the Normandy coast. It was made of old ships filled with concrete, but the *caissons*, as they were called, looked like huge black rocks now. Jutting out of the calm grey sea they looked surprisingly natural and not out of place at all.

And the beaches looked so peaceful. It was hard to imagine the tanks rolling off ships in the harbour and the soldiers running ashore. It was hard to imagine the Germans on shore, taken by surprise but ready anyway, with their massive guns. It was hard to imagine these sandy beaches covered with dead and bleeding bodies.

That evening after dinner they all helped to make a model of Arromanches and the Mulberry Harbour. They all worked on different bits of it, and most people got quite keen and laughed a lot because all the cardboard and glue reminded them of their playgroup days. Toby and Nick worked together on one of the *caissons*.

Nick seemed calmer now, Toby thought, even though Danny was making a show of himself. While everyone else got on with the model, he read aloud from the plan they were using as a guide. It was on the wall and was full of the facts he loved.

'The Mulberry Harbour had to be capable of handling 7000 tonnes of material every day. It had to be capable of being operational 15 days after the landings and to operate until the beginning of Autumn 1944.'

Mrs Irons said it had taken months of fighting to drive

the Nazis from France. They'd conquered the whole country, she reminded them, though some of the south was nominally still French. The French had to recognise them as masters. The Germans killed anyone who resisted. They killed Jews, of course, even if they didn't resist.

Danny went to bed early, thinking he'd get to sleep before the others came up. Unfortunately they crashed into the dorm soon after he'd got his head down.

'Hello, Danny! Vee haf vays of making you leaf the dorm!' Callum said, goose-stepping past his bunk. Lewis, Nick and Toby were close behind. Big George came in a few seconds later with a Hitler moustache on his upper lip. The others fell about laughing when it fell off.

Danny pulled the covers over his head and eventually the others put the lights out. He heard Callum climbing into the bunk above him. Then it went quiet thank goodness and he tried to calm down by remembering the good things that had happened that day. It had been interesting. The girls had been nice to him. Tomorrow they were going to see the Bayeux Tapestry in the morning then they were going to Arromanches, he thought. Today he'd managed to keep out of the way of this lot. He'd keep out of their way tomorrow too. Now all he had to do was sleep.

But seconds later he felt water on his face. Water was pouring down on him. He sat up – bumping his head on the bunk above – and more water came down, soaking him. Then the light came on and there was Callum's face, hanging over the edge of the bunk above.

'Oh, mein Gott! Dani-elle. I did not know it vas you. I thought it vas a toiletten. I vas haffing a piss!' He jumped down and stood in front of him, thrusting himself forward as he did up his flies. And the room exploded with laughter – Lewis's hideous giggle, Big George's bray and Callum's high-pitched yelp.

Hanging over the edge of the bunks, their faces looked like gargoyles. But the worst thing of all was seeing Toby's face among them.

10

It was better than scoring. Nick felt a rush of pleasure and pride. Callum had been brilliant. They'd all been brilliant, but he Nick Tate had master-minded it, leaving Toby out of it, for the most part because he wasn't a hundred per cent reliable yet. Toby still felt responsible for the prat – because of their family connections – and would do while he was in the same room. But that wouldn't be for long now. The prat had already run from the room. He'd be whingeing to the teachers by now, saying Callum had wee-weed over him, which he hadn't, of course. So when he returned, teacher in tow, they'd be ready for him. They would say he'd lied and prove it. Prove that he'd spilt water over himself getting a drink in the dark. And then they would ask for him to be moved to another dorm, because he'd lied to get Callum into trouble. They'd have right on their side. The teachers couldn't refuse.

Before he put out the light Nick made sure that the beaker Callum had emptied over Danny ended up in the prat's bunk. Then he lay in the darkness, waiting for a teacher to appear. Half time and his team were winning. He looked forward to the second half.

But Danny came back alone. He hadn't complained because he was far too upset to speak, and he'd been too busy washing and drying himself. He didn't know if

Callum had peed on him or not, but he felt as if he had.

Toby, on the bunk under Nick's, dreaded the teacher appearing. The water incident had been a complete surprise. Already, he couldn't believe that he'd laughed at Danny, but he had – till the tears streamed down his face. It had seemed so funny at the time.

He felt short of breath now, anxious. The others had filled him in on the plan and told him what to say but he didn't know if he could go through with it.

When he heard the door open and saw the silhouette of Danny trailing his pyjama top, he lay tensely waiting for the teacher to follow. When none did he relaxed a bit and watched Danny crawl into the dry end of his bunk and pull the duvet over his head. Then the door clicked shut and it was too dark to see anything.

He heard Callum say, 'Aren't you going to blub then? Aren't you going to report us?'

There was no reply.

Toby lay awake for a long time. If Danny had told the staff they might still come up and check things out. Was he crying? A sound which might have been a sob broke the silence once but he couldn't be sure. Outside the sea crashed against the sea wall. Inside central heating pipes gurgled and beds creaked. Were any of the others awake? Were any of them having second thoughts? When someone farted and no giggles or comments followed he concluded that everyone else was asleep.

In the morning Nick woke early and roused the others, signalling them not to wake Danny. He'd decided it would be best to get their story in first. They dressed and went down to breakfast just as the alarm clock went off.

When the alarm woke Danny he felt awful. He'd slept with the duvet stuffed in his mouth so his mouth was dry – and his eyes were sore. He was relieved to see that the others had gone, even before he recalled the previous night's events. Then he sat on the bed for a long time trying to calm himself and think straight. He wanted to tell the teachers what had happened but he didn't want to cry in front of everyone.

When he reached the dining room it was full and echoed with the sound of cheerful voices. A lot of people were already at the long tables eating, but there was a long queue at the hatch for warm croissants and hot chocolate. He sat down, near the door, the same place as yesterday. He didn't feel hungry but poured himself some water from the jug nearby.

It was a while before Mrs Taylor called out, 'Oh Danny! Good! There you are.' To his surprise, she brought him half a baguette spread with jam and a cup of chocolate, saying, 'Sorry no croissants left. We're leaving for Bayeux at 8 o'clock, but you've got time to eat this if you hurry. We let you sleep because Nick told us you had a broken night. I'd have a drink *before* you go to bed tonight, if I were you.'

What had they told her? He couldn't work it out. Whatever it was, she'd believed it.

She said, 'I expect you're looking forward to seeing the Bayeux Tapestry, aren't you?'

He didn't answer because he still thought he might

cry. Should he tell her about last night? She might believe him. All the teachers were much nicer than they were at school. They looked different too. At the other end of the table Mr O'Kelly was wearing a sweatshirt with a teddy bear on it that growled when you pressed its tummy. The girls were taking turns at pressing it and Nick Tate was saying 'Can I borrow your shirt, Sir?'

Mr O'Kelly laughed. He wasn't very tall and looked like a lot of the boys, except that he was wider. He had the same fashionable hairstyle. Everybody looked happy. If he told Mrs Taylor about last night she'd look cross again. Mrs Irons would tell him not to whinge. Nick and the others might be even nastier to him. While he was thinking Mrs Taylor went and sat down.

Toby watched anxiously when Mrs Taylor went over to Danny. Would he tell her what had really happened? What then? It was a relief when he saw her walking away.

He jumped as Nick suddenly slapped him on the back.

'I've just been talking to Kelly-O. We're going to stop at the beach on the way back for a game of footie. I've told him I think you're good enough for the first team.'

Toby saw Danny get up from the table, most of his breakfast uneaten. Nick saw Toby noticing him. 'You're not worrying about him, are you? I've told you, he's not your responsibility. Look at him, he hasn't even got the guts to complain. We'll have to think of some other way of getting rid of him.'

Then Mrs Taylor walked past saying, 'Funny child that. Just not a mixer.'

Mrs Irons shook her head and said, 'I'm afraid not.' It

was obvious who they were talking about.

Nick smirked.

Danny was leaving the dining room.

Nick mock-punched Toby's arm to get his full attention. 'I've told him to watch you, see how fast you are. *Kelly-O*. I told him you'd be good on the wing.'

Toby had longed to be in the team ever since he'd started at Lindley, but Mr O'Kelly just never seemed to be looking when he was playing well. Nick, Callum, Big George and Lewis were all in the first team.

'Come on, lads.' Mr O'Kelly was coming over to them now. 'The sooner we get the educational bit over, the sooner we get to the beach for a practice.'

Mrs Taylor said, 'I heard that, Rob.' But she laughed.

They were spending the morning in Bayeux, the afternoon at Mont St. Michel. There might be time to stop at one of the beaches for a game on the way back, she said.

They could see the cream and green Buffalo coach waiting when they stepped into the hall, because the big front doors of the château were open. It had rained in the night and the gravel on the drive looked as if it had been washed. So did the cone-shaped bushes. Seagulls mewled overhead. Ted the driver was standing at the foot of the steps in a plaid shirt with his sleeves rolled up. The weather was still amazingly summery, though there were clouds to the west, where they were heading. Some people were already on the bus.

Nick led the five musketeers aboard. Toby was just

behind him. Behind him Lewis said, 'I hope nobody's got the back seat.'

And Callum replied, 'It doesn't matter if they have.'

But somebody had got their seat, Louise and some other girls.

Nick said, 'Sorry, that's our seat. We've bagged it.'

But Louise said, 'Get lost, Nick. First come, first served. We haven't got fixed seats. We're all sitting in different places today.'

Toby noticed Danny on the seat in front of the girls, his head mostly hidden by a book.

From behind him in the gangway Big George called out, 'D'ya want anyone thumping, Nick?'

But Nick laughed and said, 'I'll see you later, Louise my girl.' It was a take-off of Mr Hall and Louise laughed too.

Out of the corner of his eye Danny watched his enemies all about-turn to face the front of the bus. Why couldn't he be like Louise? Nobody conquered her. He heard Lewis muttering to Callum, 'I thought you said Nick'd make 'em. I thought we were the Back Seat Gang.'

Callum didn't answer.

As they drove to Bayeux, Mrs Irons handed out worksheets. Then she picked up the microphone, to give them a bit of background, she said.

Danny read the worksheet. The questions were really simple – and Mrs Irons was telling them most of the answers now in her talk. She spoke to them as if they were idiots, emphasising every other word as if they didn't know anything.

'In 1066 the *Normans*, that's the French people of this part of France, *Normandy*, invaded England. Their leader was Duke William of Normandy who had a claim to the English throne. So he got together a fleet and landed on the south coast of England. And they fought King Harold, the Saxon king of England at the *Battle of Hastings!* Now who won?'

'We won. We won. We won the war!' Big George sounded as if he was at a football match and a few people laughed.

'Not this time,' said Mrs Irons. 'Well, it depends what you mean by "we" of course.'

Froggy Lewis, sitting next to Toby, sniggered.

'What do the rest of you think?'

Nobody answered. Danny could have but still didn't trust his voice.

The others didn't think anything, it was obvious. No wonder she spoke to them as if they were idiots. They were idiots. She had to tell them the simplest things. Then she told them wrong. William of Normandy *didn't* have a very good claim to the throne. He'd forced poor Harold to promise to let him have it. Poor Harold had been thrown into a dungeon and William wouldn't let him out till he promised him the throne of England. What sort of promise was that? William was a big bully – like a lot of people he could mention – and he carried on bullying the Saxons when he was king. He took their food and land from them. He forced them to build castles for his followers. He even forced them to use the French language.

'The *Normans* won,' Mrs Irons went on. 'William the *Conqueror* beat Harold, King of England, who was shot through the eye by a Norman arrow. Then William became William I of England.'

It looked as if the bullies always won.

The battle and events leading up to it were all depicted on the Bayeux Tapestry, Mrs Irons said, from the Norman point of view, of course. Bishop Odo of Bayeux, who was William's step-brother had had it embroidered by the women of Bayeux. Danny leaned forward to hear better because by now some people were talking. Some were even yawning. Mrs Irons didn't seem to notice. Like most teachers she was blind most of the time. She said they would need twenty francs if they wanted to hire headphones with a commentary.

Toby, glancing back, saw Danny listening avidly. Others had noticed him too, and hung out their tongues in a mockery of his rapt expression. Stupid Danny, to show how eager he was about history. He'd never learned that laid-back was cool.

Suddenly Nick who was just behind, said, 'Tell you what, Tobe, let's give your Danny a chance.'

'W-what d'you mean?' Nick sounded almost kind and Toby couldn't help feeling suspicious.

'We'll give him a double dog dare,' said Nick.

They played dare games sometimes, usually on wet breaks when they couldn't play football. They'd play truth and dare, or simply dare someone to kiss one of the uglier girls or write a swear word on the blackboard, something like that. If the person didn't do it they'd have to pay a forfeit. A double dog dare was a really hard dare. Once they'd dared Kev Walsh to smash the fire alarm. He'd done it, of course.

'Like what?' said Toby.

'I'll think of something, and if he does it we'll let him stay in the dorm. Okay?'

Toby didn't answer and Nick closed his eyes to think.

Toby thought about it too, and wanted to ask if they'd let Danny stay and be okay to him if he did the dare. Then he decided he'd be wasting his breath. Danny wouldn't do it. He wasn't that sort of daft. Nick's lips were twitching as if he could barely suppress a smile, and after a second or two he got up and whispered something to Callum and Big George who were sharing a seat. Then he went to the back where Danny was sitting alone and sat by him.

When he came back he said, 'I dared him to miss the coach going back to Brion sur Mer and make his own way back to the centre. He said he'd think about it.'

In fact Danny hadn't said anything to Nick. He'd hardly heard what he said, he was concentrating so hard at looking out of the window. He didn't want to talk to Nick, and they'd arrived at Bayeux which seemed really nice. The streets were cobbled and full of historical buildings, built from huge blocks of grey stone. He wondered which one was the museum. There were posters and banners and signposts all over the place, but they were going too fast for him to read them.

Nick seemed to want Toby's approval.

'It'd give him a good scare, but he wouldn't come to any

88

harm. He's sure to have learned all that *Je me suis perdu* stuff.'

They had all had to learn to say 'I'm lost' in French, and they all had identity cards to hand to a gendarme if they did get separated from the group. The cards had their names on and the name of the centre where they were staying.

'But it's impossible to miss the bus,' Toby said. 'Mrs Taylor always calls the register to check that we're all there and she does a head-count.'

'So *someone* will answer when his name's called,' said Nick smiling.

Toby didn't worry too much. Danny wouldn't accept the dare. His daftness took other forms, making himself conspicuous for instance.

They'd only just left the coachpark and were still walking in convoy past the cathedral, when he started. Or rather stopped – suddenly – because he saw a water wheel in the grounds of a building they were passing. Mrs Taylor nearly tripped over him and any normal person would have apologised profusely, but Danny said, 'Look at the droplets, Mrs Taylor. *Look at the droplets.*' Sunlight made the water sparkle as the wheel went round.

He had no idea how daft he sounded. He didn't notice the people near him making screw-loose signs.

Nick said, 'Let's get away from the nerd before we're all arrested.'

They all split up then, but Danny managed to embarrass them all again soon after they were inside the museum. They'd just stepped into the narrow gallery where the tapestry was displayed in an illuminated case along the left-hand side, when Danny's hired headphones fell off. Several people had hired them – they said the commentary was really good – but only Danny's managed to fall off. And he just stood there, the broken bits at his feet, blocking the way. Fortunately, an official took pity on him and got him a new set.

The tapestry was worth seeing. It was better than most people expected and like a colourful cartoon strip. Red, brown, gold and blue were the main colours, with black highlights and it was very clear. The English soldiers all had black hair and black moustaches and the Normans were clean shaven so you could tell who was doing what and follow the battle. Some bits were better than others, of course. There were seventy metres of it after all, but the horses really did look as if they were galloping and the battle scenes were brilliant. The arrows seemed to whizz. It was hard to believe it was nine hundred years old.

Danny, of course, was enraptured.

It wasn't long before Toby heard Big George say, 'Look at the prat.'

And there was Danny scrutinising one little bit – though it only showed three men sitting at a table – and he was declaiming. Toby immediately realised why. He'd seen some of his beloved Latin.

'Episcopus Odo benedicit prandium,' he said. Then he translated it, possibly for the benefit of Rachel who was standing nearby, possibly not. He was utterly absorbed. 'Bishop Odo blessed the meal!'

'Is that really what it says?' Rachel seemed impressed.

Nick said. 'Odo? *He's* oddo!' And everyone near him laughed, even Mr O'Kelly.

Toby looked for the doors. Danny was his own worst enemy.

'The big girl,' said Nick, suddenly by his side. 'Still want to be his friend?'

Mr O'Kelly said, 'Remember, you lot, you've got half an hour here to do your worksheets, then five minutes in the gift shop.'

'Half an hour! I've seen all I want already!' Big George headed for the doors at the end and Toby followed. The doors opened into a large gift shop full of expensive things. There were piles of videos, books, embroidery sets, jigsaws and table mats all decorated with scenes from the Bayeux Tapestry and a lot of jewellery in a glass case. Toby saw a jigsaw that his mum would have liked but it was way out of his price range. Two American men were the only customers. Feeling an assistant looking at him suspiciously, Toby bought a couple of postcards and wished he hadn't rushed out of the gallery. He hadn't seen half of the tapestry, and he hadn't answered any of the questions on his worksheet. But you couldn't go back in unless you went outside again, and found the entrance on the other side of the courtyard. Even then you might have to pay again. He was wishing the others would come soon when George said, 'There's nothing worth pinching. Let's go. I saw a better place.'

He grabbed Toby's arm and led the way out into the courtyard. and then under a stone arch, into a narrow road where there was another gift shop with lots of things outside. Toby bought a tea towel for his mum and a pencil for Polly. It had a rubber arrow on the end and he thought she'd like it. By the time they got back to the museum some of the others were standing outside with Mr O'Kelly. Several girls were unfurling paper friezes of the tapestry but most people hadn't bought anything. Big George told them about the other shop and Mr O'Kelly said they could go if they liked and then back to the coach. They were leaving at 12.00. Toby and Big George showed them the way.

Nick and Callum and several others were still in the museum shop with Mrs Irons and Mrs Taylor who was trying to sort out a bit of bother. Unfortunately the shop had sold out of the friezes that most of the girls wanted and an assistant had gone off to look for some more. But when she came back one of the girls said she'd paid and the assistant said she hadn't. Mrs Taylor told her to check the till, but the assistant said she couldn't, so Mrs Taylor had sent for the manager. And Mrs Taylor got her way. The manager checked the till and the Lindley girl was proved right. Sweeping out, Mrs Taylor didn't check to see if anyone was still in the gallery. Nor did anyone else. Nick and Callum were among those congratulating her on her triumph. If they knew that Danny was still inside, they didn't say so.

When Mrs Taylor called the register just before they set off from the car park at 12.05 everyone answered. When she counted heads there were exactly forty. She didn't notice the coming and going at the back.

11

At one o'clock a gallery official asked Danny to leave because the gallery was closing for lunch. By this time the coach was on the way to Mont St. Michel, but Danny didn't know this. He didn't know that the others had left nearly an hour earlier, and he thought the coach would be where he had left it.

He managed to find his way back to the coachpark. When he couldn't see the green and cream coach where he expected, in the middle quite near a framed Plan de Ville, he began to look elsewhere, trying not to get run over by the coaches leaving or arriving. There were several now. He'd thought the cream coach with its buffalo logo was quite distinctive, but now a lot looked similar. So he started to peer inside the stationary ones, hoping to see some familiar faces. When he didn't, he went back to the museum, thinking he'd find one of the teachers standing by the entrance, waiting for him. By this point he was feeling rather nervous. He thought the teacher would be annoyed with him. But the teacher wasn't there. There was no one there at all and there was a barrier across the archway entrance.

The museum had closed. And the coach had gone.

As his stomach began to churn Danny tried to keep calm. He mustn't panic. He mustn't. Slowly he pieced together what must have happened. He remembered

Nick Tate's saying something about a dare. Nick Tate had obviously planned this, like he planned what happened in the dorm last night. But the others had helped him. Toby had helped him. Tears came into Danny's eyes. He tried to push them back in. He mustn't think about last night. He must think about what to do.

He'd learned what to do. He'd learned phrases for homework. What were they? At least he was on his own. That was a good thing. He was better on his own. There was no one to hassle him. Standing in the empty street he tried to recall the lesson on what to do in an emergency.

Find a gendarme! That was it. He must say, '*Je me suis perdu. Aidez-moi, s'il vous plaît.*' That was it. I am lost. Help me please. Then he must show the gendarme his identity card. It had his name and the name and address of the study centre on it. The gendarme would contact the centre. Someone would get him back there. Nobody could be lost for long, Mrs Taylor had assured their parents.

'*Je me suis perdu. Aidez-moi, s'il vous plaît.*'

'*Je me suis perdu. Aidez-moi, s'il vous plaît.*'

Danny said it over and over again as he searched his pockets for his identity card.

Meanwhile the coach with the Lindley party aboard, was heading south-west along the D572. As Danny realised he'd left his identity card in his bag, *and* that he hadn't got his bag – where had he left that? – Mrs Taylor was telling the party that Mont St. Michel was a tiny, picturesque island, joined to the mainland by a narrow causeway. When they got there they could explore in groups of three or four and they could buy their own lunch. She could recommend the crêpes. There were lots of things to see, she said, the ancient castle and church at the top of the mont and hundreds of shops and cafés on the way up. She told them to sort out who they were going with now. When Nick went to the front and asked her, very politely in French, if he and his mates could be a cinq Mrs Taylor smiled and said yes, as long as they were sensible and did frequent head-counts. They must all do frequent head-counts, she said, to make sure no one was missing. They were responsible for each other. They must all be back at the bus by four before the tide came in. That was very important because when the tide came in Mont St. Michel got completely cut off. She had timed things carefully.

No one mentioned the missing Danny. No one seemed to notice that he was missing.

Toby wondered about him, briefly, when he found himself standing near Louise and Rachel in the car park. He started to say, 'Isn't Danny with you?' – because, well, who else would have him? But the girls didn't seem to hear his question. They were looking up at the mont, saying that it was bigger than they'd expected. It *was* bigger and darker than Toby thought it would be, and standing in its shadow he couldn't suppress a shiver. Rachel turned to look at him, but before he could ask about Danny, Nick grabbed his arm and Callum rushed by saying, 'Last one to the top's a plonker!' Big George and Lewis were close behind.

It wasn't long before Toby was puffing. Mont St.

Michel really was a mountain, with thousands of steps carved out of the granite. Nick led the way up, weaving through the maze of pathways, dodging tourists and their dogs, negotiating alleyways till fit as he was, even he was puffed out. Then they all stopped – they must have been about halfway up – to buy some of the famous pancakes. They ate them in an outdoor café looking over the ramparts at the swirling currents making channels in the quicksands hundreds of feet beneath them. Then Lewis saw a notice which said traitors had been thrown from those ramparts, and as they looked it seemed to Toby that the mud heaved like a monster, waiting for some victim to be thrown to it.

He said so and Big George grabbed Lewis. 'Over you go! Splat!'

'Splonk!' said Lewis, miming a body fighting for its life in the sucking mud. They all fell about laughing. Then the garçon arrived with their bill.

Miles away, still in Bayeux, Danny was beginning to panic. Realising he'd left his bag in the museum he'd ducked under the barrier and gone up to the closed door. A notice said:

FERMÉ.
De 13.00h à 15.00h.

Closed for two hours! '

'*Je me suis perdu. Aidez-moi, s'il vous plaît.*'

He kept repeating the phrases as he looked for the gendarmerie. He thought he knew where it was – from the Plan de Ville – but didn't come to it. In fact he seemed to have walked away from the town centre. There were even fewer people around now and the few shops he saw all had FERMÉ on them.

Boulangerie. FERMÉ.

Patisserie. FERMÉ. Some were closed for one hour, some for two which was a pity because he was hungry. One restaurant was open, but he only had a few coins in his pocket, not enough money for a proper meal.

'*Je me suis perdu. Aidez-moi, s'il vous plaît.*'

He was scared to stop saying it, in case he forgot it completely. But there was no one to help him. Bayeux, on a Wednesday lunchtime in late October was like a ghost town. The streets were empty, because the French people were all inside their houses, eating proper French lunches. Looking down the tree-lined streets, at all the closed doors, reminded him of the first night of the holiday. Of walking down the empty corridor. Of seeing all the closed doors. They were closed because people didn't want him. Nobody wanted him in their room.

Why didn't anyone want him? It was a question he'd begun to ask himself a lot lately. Why did everyone else have friends? Why didn't he have friends? What was wrong with him?

Catching sight of his reflection in a shop window, he stopped for a moment and examined it. Did he have two heads? Did he have some terrible skin disease that people were afraid of catching? Did he smell?

Toby didn't think about Danny again till the musketeers got back to the coach a good quarter of an hour before the deadline – so they could regain the back seat. Ted was already there, reading an old copy of the *Sun* and he let them on. From his corner Toby watched the rest of the party return but didn't see Danny. Then he realised that he hadn't seen him all afternoon, though he'd seen almost everyone else, including the teachers.

Mrs Taylor began to call the register. When she got to Danny's name he answered in French. Quite a few people were answering in French or Franglais by this time so that wasn't unusual. But where was he? Toby stood up to look round, but hands pulled him down, laughing. Mrs Taylor began to count heads. After the back row had been counted Callum crouched down on the floor.

Mrs Taylor said, 'I'll have to count again. I only made it 39.'

At which point Callum stood up and Nick called out, 'You missed Callum, Mrs Taylor. He was doing up his laces.'

Then he said to Toby, 'See, he's okay. Don't worry about him. You're not in the Infants now. And nor is he.'

'But where . . . '

'I said, *don't* worry. He knows the drill, and he speaks French *beau-ti-fully*.' Nick spoke the last word in a phoney French accent.

Someone said, 'Ooh aah. Cantona!'

Lewis giggled and said, 'He must have accepted your dare, Nick.'

The others laughed again.

The coach was swinging out of the car park now. The sun had gone in and clouds were gathering over Mont

St. Michel. It looked darker than ever. Mrs Taylor's voice crackled over the microphone. 'Settle down now. All being well, we should be back at the centre by six-thirty. In the time before dinner fill in your diaries and complete the questions in your workbooks if you haven't already done so. Then smarten yourselves up for *le diner* at seven.'

Someone said, 'Aren't we going to stop for a game of footie on the way back?'

Mr O'Kelly stood up and said, 'Sorry, lads. We haven't time today but there might be time tomorrow when we go to the beach at Arromanches.'

But that's where Danny was because he'd seen a signpost pointing to it, and it had jogged his memory, he thought. He thought the school party was going there – to see the famous beach where the Allies had landed. It was only nine kilometres away, He worked it out. That was just over five miles. He could walk that easily in about two hours. He'd walked further than that in Derbyshire.

So at just gone two o'clock he'd set off.

12

He enjoyed the walk, but then he always enjoyed walking. The road meandered – he liked that word – and once he'd left Bayeux, it meandered through pleasant countryside, uphill but gently so. Rather like English countryside in fact, except for the different styled houses in the villages. They were mostly three-storeys high with funny grey roofs which came down the sides, and they had lots of shutters like all French houses.

Getting into a rhythm, he swung his arms as he walked, on the left-hand side facing the traffic. Not that there was a lot of that. Just the occasional tractor or car. That's why he preferred the country to the town. It wasn't so fast so you didn't have to think of so many things at the same time. On either side of him were hedges, some with ripe blackberries, but he didn't stop to eat any. He just kept moving. He didn't want to break his rhythm. He was heading for Arromanches.

Left right.

Left right.

Ploughed fields to one side. Meadows with beige cows on the other.

Left right.

Left right.

On both sides were sloping trees, leafless on the seaward side, and leafy on the other. The trees leaned towards him and the blue sky arched above him – a celestial dome! Walking made him feel better. It calmed him down. It always did. He would soon meet the others.

Left right.

Left right.

What a surprise they would get when they saw him.

Arromanches 5 kilometres.

He was nearly halfway already.

Arromanches 3 kilometres.

It was satisfying passing the mile-stones, *kilometre-*stones he corrected himself, each one with a lower number on than the last. He was doing well, aiding himself! He didn't need a gendarme to aid him which was just as well because he didn't see any. When the land started to rise more steeply he slowed down a bit, but by half past three he was on a crest – and there below him not too far away was the sea!

Arromanches, it must be! For there were the *caissons*, like a huge capital E that had fallen apart. There was the Mulberry Harbour!

When he set off again, downhill now, so he was much faster, the sea-view disappeared for a bit, but he saw it again later when he reached the top of another crest, and at four o'clock exactly he reached Arromanches!

Stopping for a moment he leaned against the road sign to consider. Straight ahead of him was a narrow road called Cale Eisenhower which went down to the beach. Swinging to the right was the main road leading to the town centre.

Weren't the others going to play football on the

beach? He headed for it and there were the *caissons*. Close up, they made him think of beached whales, their flesh rotted away, though they were made of old iron ships. He thought of the men who had died on D-day. 410,000 Allied soldiers had landed on the Normandy beaches. 10,000 had died on that one day.

Suddenly he realised how quiet it was. He was all alone on a sandy beach which seemed to stretch for miles, and all he could hear was the sea sighing. Till a sea-bird broke the silence and then he noticed a couple of figures further along, with a dog. They threw sticks for it from time to time. He zipped up his anorak. A wind had got up bringing in dark clouds from the sea.

Pulling up his anorak hood, he turned to face the sea wall which curved round the beach like a big C. The town was at the other end. And so was a huge crucifix which dominated the skyline. Thinking he could see some coaches in the town, he headed for them, walking purposefully along the top of the sea wall. The coach, that's what he must find now, before it got dark.

The coaches, two of them, were in front of the Musée de Débarquement, the D-day Museum which over-looked the beach at Arromanches. The museum formed one side of the town square, the beach another and there were shops and cafés on the other two sides. But Danny saw hardly any of this. Dismayed that neither of the coaches was the Lindley High coach, he pressed on. He'd spotted more coaches on the promontory overlooking the town, near the base of the giant crucifix, and he was heading for them, So he didn't notice how

English everything round him seemed, how friendly and welcoming. The cafés had names like Winston's and Monty's Bar and there were lots of signs saying WELCOME TO OUR LIBERATORS. They'd been put up for the fiftieth anniversary in 1994. If Danny had stopped and asked for help he'd have got it. Almost anyone would have been glad to help a lost English boy.

But Danny didn't stop. He hurried through the town, keeping the crucifix as a landmark. Soon he was climbing the path to the coachpark he'd seen. It was outside a round building, with ARROMANCHES 360 written on it. Unfortunately the Lindley coach wasn't in the car park. The other coaches had gone. Anxious now – would he ever find the others? – he didn't notice an old man hurrying out of the round building. But he went to see what it was – a cinema showing film of the D-day landings according to the information on the glass doors. In French and English, it said that nine synchronised cameras projected original footage onto nine screens and the audience stood in the middle, seeing, hearing and *feeling* what it was really like as the battle raged. Were the others inside watching? With the wind whipping round him, Danny tried to think calmly, and again remembered Mr O'Kelly saying they'd have a game of football on the beach.

So he went to the edge of the cliff and looked down, leaning on a safety rail. Below him there *were* people playing footie on the sand, children he thought, finding it hard because the wind kept lifting the ball and carrying it away. A few shouts reached him. English shouts, he thought, so he set off again, towards the path he'd just climbed.

And he tripped. Fell full length – didn't know if a stone or a tussock of grass had caused it. Just knew that when he tried to get up it was agony.

He must have cried out, because when he looked up he saw an old man coming towards him, half crouching and looking all around him. Suddenly he was kneeling at Danny's feet, examining his ankle.

'*Bonjour. Comment vous appellez-vous?*' he muttered without looking up.

All Danny could see was a brown skull beneath a stubble of white hair.

'*Je m'appelle Danny Lamb,*' he replied automatically, programmed by hundreds of French lessons.

'*L'agneau?*' The old man thrust out his hand and Danny shook it. '*Renard. Mais ne vous inquiétez pas,*' he said, thrusting his hand in his trouser pocket, and bringing out a folded ruler. Was Renard the old man's name? Danny wasn't quite sure what he had heard after the first question, but tried to translate as he watched the old man untie the red and white scarf at his neck. Then he was binding the scarf round the ruler and his hurt ankle, with quick competent movements. Suddenly he moved to Danny's side, held out his arm and said, '*Allons! Vite!*'

And Danny obeyed because it didn't occur to him not to. Only later did the words stranger danger come into his head. The man spoke with authority and Danny found himself getting to his feet, with the old man's help.

'*Vite!*' urged the old man.

Danny hopped along, putting the weight on his good foot, his arm round the old man's shoulders. Renard – if that was his name – wasn't much taller than Danny, who could now see an old 2CV in the car park. It was like his mother's except that it was grey and older. It was the only vehicle there. Perhaps the old man would take him to the hospital? He had done good First Aid already.

'*Je – me – suis – perdu.*' He remembered the words at last. '*Aidez-moi, s'il vous plaît.*'

The old man grunted. His shirt near Danny's nose smelled of sweat and garlic. They reached the car. '*Entrez,*' said the old man opening the passenger door.

Danny got in and the old man darted round to the other side.

'*À l'hôpital?*' said Danny but his words were drowned by the car engine roaring into action. He clung to the door handle as the car lurched forward. Realising there were no seatbelts, he now began to regret getting into the car. The man was a terrible driver and hadn't switched on the lights though it was getting dark outside. The horizon was red but the rest of the sky was purplish grey like a bruise.

'*Vous avez...ssss...orme. Bon.*'

He couldn't understand what the man was saying, even when he suddenly spoke in heavily accented English, 'You 'ave 'idden ze uniform, yes?'

It still didn't make sense. They were in the country now. Fields stretched out on either side, mostly bare earth, some full of spiky artichoke plants. So he wasn't taking him to a hospital. So where were they going?

They passed a road sign, but too fast for Danny to read it.

Then he cried out, 'Ouch!' as Renard took a sudden right turn up a track, and his hurt foot banged against the side of the car. And the old man went mad.

'*Zut! Dites "zut" pas "Oush!" Pas un mot d'anglais.*'

Not one word of English? Danny understood that. But why on earth not? As the rutted track stretched out in front of them, then disappeared into the shadows, he wondered again where Renard was taking him. And he noticed something odd about the brown hands which gripped the steering wheel. Renard had no thumbs. Suddenly Danny was filled with foreboding.

When Toby realised Danny wasn't on the coach at Mont St. Michel he wanted to go to the front and tell the staff. He said so, but Nick shook his head and murmured, 'No point, Tobe. He'll be at the centre by now.'

Big George said, 'You keep quiet, okay?'

Nick put his finger over his lips like an infant school teacher. 'Don't worry about it. Danny will have had all afternoon to get back. He'll have learnt all that *Je me suis perdu* stuff and given his *carte d'identité* to a nice gendarme by now. He might even have been rushed back in a *gendarme's* car. He'll like that.'

All afternoon! When had Danny gone missing then? Nobody would tell him. Big George was dealing out cards. Toby couldn't concentrate on Black Jack. He couldn't help thinking about Danny, all on his own. He was even more worried when they arrived at the centre and it became clear that he wasn't there. Right up to the last minute he hoped that the others had been joking, that he would see Danny getting off the coach, or waiting for them in the entrance hall.

Danny didn't get off the coach.

He wasn't in the entrance hall.

Surely Nick would tell someone now?

But Nick led the way up to the dorm. When the door was closed he said they'd notice Danny's absence at dinner time if he hadn't appeared by then.

Danny hadn't appeared by then and as the five of them sat down in the dining room, Nick took a concerned look. Then he said quite loudly, 'Oh dear, Danny doesn't seem to be here.'

Then he went to Mrs Taylor who was sitting with the other teachers at the end of the table. Toby saw him, the image of responsibility, telling the teacher who frowned as she stood up and surveyed the room.

Then she said, 'He must still be in the dormitory. Go and tell him, Nick, please.'

And Nick shook his head sadly. 'Sorry, Mrs Taylor. We've been in the dorm since we got back, filling in our diaries. He didn't come up there. We thought he must have gone to the activities room.'

She looked annoyed. 'Go and have a look there, will you?'

'Okay,' said Nick. 'He's probably got his head in a book and didn't notice the time.'

Big George and Lewis could hardly contain their glee.

They were kicking each other under the table. Callum just stared at Toby.

When Nick came back saying he couldn't find Danny, Mrs Taylor said, 'Strange.'

Then she got the register from her bag. Only Danny didn't answer when she called all their names. Mr O'Kelly went off, saying he'd look in the boys' loos.

Mrs Taylor said, 'Think carefully, everyone. Who's seen Danny since we got back? He can't be far.'

No one answered.

She said, 'He was definitely on the coach coming back from Mont St. Michel. I've ticked his name. So let's go back a bit further. Who was sitting near him? We didn't leave him sleeping on the coach, did we?'

Slightly agitated she prompted, 'Someone must have been near him, behind or in front of him or across the aisle. Now think.'

When there was no reply Mrs Irons said, 'Who went round with him at Mont St. Michel? Somebody must have. You were in threes at least, remember.'

There was no reply to this either.

Mrs Taylor said crossly, 'You're not telling us that no one went round with Danny?'

Then Mr O'Kelly came back saying Danny was nowhere in the building as far as he could see. The three teachers looked at the class, then at one another, and Toby saw their faces change, saw worry and irritation turn to dismay as they realised Danny had been missing for some time.

Mrs Taylor almost whined, 'But he said, *Oui,*

madame when I called the register. I remember.'

'Or someone did,' said Mr O'Kelly. His eyes swept round the room and Toby felt himself go red.

'I heard him too,' said Mrs Irons. 'I didn't imagine it.' There was a trace of panic in her voice now. 'We *can't* have left him at Mont St. Michel.' But she obviously thought they had.

In another room a phone rang.

Toby was thinking of saying that Danny wasn't at Mont St. Michel, when Rachel cried out, '*We* should have looked after him! We should have *thought*!' She obviously meant Louise and herself. Some of the other girls huddled round them and said it wasn't their fault.

Madame Bleu appeared in the doorway and Mrs Taylor and Mrs Irons left the room. Mr O'Kelly told everyone to start eating the hors d'oeuvres but didn't eat anything himself. Some people ate a bit of bread but the *saucisson* and grated carrot had hardly been touched when Mrs Irons came back. She said there had been a telephone call from the security staff at the museum saying they'd found Danny's bag, with his carte d'identité in it.

When Mrs Taylor returned, she looked quite ill, seemed to have shrunk in fact. She said the police had been informed and a search would begin.

Toby followed Nick to the hatch when he went to get the main course, to get him on his own. He wanted to know *where* Danny had been left, and to suggest that they tell the teachers, so the search could start in the right place

109

at least. Toby still couldn't believe that Danny had accepted Nick's dare. But Nick ignored Toby's questions.

He just said loudly, 'Poor old Danny. I wonder where he's got to.'

Then he made his way back to the table saying, 'Mind out of the way, Andrea, if you don't want *poulet* down your neck!'

In the dorm before dinner he'd briefed them all to act normally, to show concern, but definitely not let on that they'd noticed Danny's absence earlier. Toby hadn't said anything then, because he didn't know what to say. He still didn't know what had happened. Nobody had told him. He knew he ought to say something. But it was impossible to get through to Nick. He seemed to be on a high.

Nick's pulses were racing. This was turning out even better than he'd planned. The nerd was out there somewhere in the dark. Losing his carte d'identité made it even harder for him. He'd be shit scared. *And* Mrs Taylor would give him hell when he turned up. If he turned up. They'd have to be careful though. Already Kelly-O suspected foul play. So would the police if they started investigating. And Toby would blab if the questioning got tough. He was almost as weak and watery as his ex-friend. The others knew they mustn't say anything. Danny Lamb was a prat. This was his own fault.

Toby didn't manage to get Nick on his own till after dinner, when they were on their way to the activities room.

110

He said, 'You've got to tell them, Nick.' It didn't go down well.

Nick said, 'What about this quiz then? What's your strongest subject?' A General Knowledge Quiz was the evening's activity. Then out of the corner of his mouth he said, 'Shut *up.*'

And the others who had caught up heard him.

Big George said, 'Toby Woby Worry Arse bothering you, Nick?'

Nick looked really mad.

Big George went on, 'You don't need to worry about Toby Woby Worry Arse, Nick.' He tweaked Toby's ear. 'If Toby Woby Worry Arse says anything, *anything*, we'll all say *he* answered for Danny Boy when the register was called both times. *He* sent Danny's mummy the nasty letter, and *he* was very, very nasty to Danny. We were shocked. We thought he was Danny's friend.'

As Callum, Big George and Lewis all nodded, Nick felt proud. The lads would stand by him. He was captain of a winning team. There was nothing to worry about. He put his arm round Toby and said, 'It looks as if you'd better stick with us, Tobe. All for one and one for all. Remember? Now let's see if our team can win even without your Danny!'

As they made their way into the activities room where the tables were arranged round the sides of the room, with the quizmaster's between them, Toby felt sick. He was stitched up. The others had thought this all out – to cover themselves if need be and leave him in the shit.

He longed for Danny to return.

13

Danny wondered if he'd ever see his family again. The old man, Renard – if that was his name – drove like a madman, gripping the wheel with his thumbless hands, sometimes half-standing to check the mirror as if he thought someone was following them. And he moved his head from left to right scanning the fields by the track. Several times he nearly went into the ditch.

Like a madman.

There was something weird about him, Danny thought, as he watched the countryside flash by, desperately trying to memorise landmarks. But this was getting harder. The sun had sunk below the horizon. The arching sky was a grey lid now, descending rapidly. Soon it would be completely dark.

As always he hated himself for thinking so slowly. A more quick-thinking person would never have got into this mess.

Renard the fox.

Agneau the lamb.

Danny's brain chugged and whirred and as the meaning of the French words came into his head they reminded him of something, but he couldn't think what.

'*Ne vous inquiétez pas, mon ami.*' Suddenly the old man touched Danny's knee with a thumbless hand, breaking into his thoughts. He'd slowed down too. Was he going to stop? Peering into the darkness at some trees ahead, Danny translated his words – *Don't worry, my friend* – and at first felt relieved that Renard had called him friend. But then looking down at the old man's fingers still on his knee, another feeling took over as other thoughts hit him suddenly. News flashes and newspaper reports and parental warnings flooded his brain. *Don't go off with strange men.*

As the car stopped Renard said something and Danny searched his face for some clue of what he was going to do. But the old man got out of the car.

Danny couldn't move. Couldn't speak. Now paralysed with fear, he could just make out a building surrounded by trees and bushes. Could see Renard opening a door and disappearing inside. And a few minutes later some cracks of light appeared. Then Renard came back to the car, and helped Danny out of it.

Inside the building, which was nothing more than a shack, Danny sat on the only chair while Renard moved around holding a rusty oil lamp. Surely he didn't live here, though he might have once. There was a table, a fireplace, and a boarded-up window, all filthy. And the floor was earth with weeds growing in it near the door. It smelled like a cave.

'*Un moment.*' Opening the door carefully, the old man went outside, holding a blackened pan that he'd found in the fireplace.

Should he run for it now? Hide somewhere? At last these thoughts did cross Danny's mind. But they were stupid thoughts. He couldn't run. His foot hurt too much and he had no idea where to run to.

As Renard came in again, Danny saw that it was now completely dark outside.

'*Café?*' There was water in the pan now and the old man set about lighting a fire with some sticks. He gave up a few minutes later. Everything was far too damp.

'*Fatigué?*' he said next.

Danny tried to think, tried to translate.

'*Et vous avez faim, bien sûr!*'

As carefully as before – as if checking that no one was watching – the old man opened the door and went out again. He came back with a baguette.

'*Mangez. Pardon. C'est tout.*' He shrugged his shoulders. '*La guerre.*'

La guerre. For the first time for several minutes Danny understood a word. *Guerre* meant war. He'd seen the word all over Normandy. As Danny ate baguette ravenously to his surprise, though he'd eaten hardly anything all that day – he thought about what the man had just said. He was trying to light the fire again, with no more success. It wasn't surprising. There was moss growing on the wooden table.

La guerre. Danny heard Renard's words again. They echoed in his head and he translated them. *Eat. Sorry. That's all. The war.*

Renard. Agneau. Fox! Lamb!

Something connected in Danny's brain! The Resistance. He had been reading a book about it on the journey to France. One group had used animal names as covers for their real names. Fox and lamb! Did Renard

114

the fox think he, Danny, was another agent? A wounded English airman perhaps?

'*Buvez.*' Now Renard was offering him a drink – of red wine from a filthy cup. He'd given up on the coffee. And Danny took it, and drank it, though it tasted like vinegar, because he thought it might act as a painkiller. His head and foot now throbbed with pain.

The old man went outside again but came back quite soon with a ladder and an old rifle. Propping the ladder against a beam, he climbed up and pushed open a trap door in the roof.

'*Il faut monter. Il faut vous cacher.*'

Danny got the message. He must climb the ladder and hide in the attic.

As an aeroplane went over the old man listened intently. '*Vite.*' Danny understood that too. There was no point in arguing. What if the old man decided he was someone else, a German even? Aware of the rifle round his neck, Danny obeyed, clinging to the ladder and pulling himself up, with the old man behind him, doing his best to protect his dangling foot. The attic was full of straw.

'*Couvrez-vous.*' Renard mimed covering himself with it and once again Danny obeyed. Then the old man descended, taking the lamp with him. Then after removing the ladder, he closed the trap door and Danny was alone in total darkness. A few minutes later he heard the car driving away.

The quiz had hardly begun when Madame Bleu came

into the activities room with two gendarmes. In their high peaked képis, with revolvers at their waists, they looked more like soldiers than policemen. The elder of the two was smoking and the smell of Gauloises reached the back of the room where Toby, flanked by Nick and Callum, was sitting. Immediately Mrs Taylor got up, leaving Mr O'Kelly in the quizmaster's seat, but he didn't ask any more questions. Mrs Taylor was soon jabbering away in French to the older officer, who was recording everything she said. He'd put a small recorder on the table near them. They all saw Mrs Taylor give him a photo of Danny. The other officer who had a Hitlerish moustache stared at them all, one by one. Every now and again the older officer shot a glance at someone too. It was very unnerving and they all kept quiet.

Then Mrs Taylor said, 'Listen, everyone,' though they were listening already. 'It now seems likely that Danny was left at Bayeux, not Mont St. Michel, but to be sure we need you all to think carefully. Think about where you were sitting on the coach. Think about who was near you, not just on the same seat, but who was behind you, in front of you or across the aisle from you.'

She paused then continued, 'Now who remembers seeing Danny on the coach?'

No one remembered.

'But *somebody* answered when I called his name, just as they did at Mont St. Michel.' She was obviously very stressed and pulled at a curl of her ginger hair as she spoke. 'I'd like to know who that was. Who? Who answered?'

116

There was a silence of about half a minute while both officers gave them searching stares.

Mrs Taylor smiled weakly and said, 'Even if it was a joke, say so. I'm sure no one meant any harm.'

Then the older gendarme murmured something to her and she murmured something back. Then more silence, more hard stares. Toby waited for Nick or Callum, George or Lewis to confess. One of them must have said it. Surely they couldn't keep quiet for much longer. But they said nothing and feeling the gendarme's eyes on him, Toby felt himself going red.

Rachel put up her hand saying quickly, 'It wasn't me. I just wanted to say that I remember Danny getting behind everyone else in the museum. He was so interested in all the Latin words round the edges of the tapestry. I was with him at first but I w-went off...'

She broke off in tears.

'Who remembers Danny coming out of the museum?' said Mrs Taylor. Nobody did.

'He's probably still there, translating all that Latin!' laughed Callum, but stopped suddenly as Nick gave him a hard kick. But it was obvious that the gendarme was asking Mrs Taylor what Callum had said.

Then they heard a phone ringing. Madame Bleu went out to answer it. She came back a few seconds later, and Mrs Irons went out with her.

When Mrs Irons came back she looked even more anxious than when she'd left the room. She said something to Mrs Taylor and handed her a piece of paper. Mrs Taylor read it, several times it seemed.

The gendarme spoke to her and she handed him the paper. She spoke to him in French. Then she turned to face the class. Even before she spoke Toby knew what she was going to say. So did Nick.

'Someone here doesn't like Danny, do they?' she said. 'His mother is very worried about him. Somebody wrote to her and said Danny wouldn't be having a nice time. We'd like to know who wrote her that letter.'

Everybody kept quiet.

Then Nick said, 'Mrs Taylor, isn't it more likely that someone who didn't come on the trip wrote the letter. Someone who wanted the place perhaps. Or someone who wasn't allowed to come on the trip.'

He was trying to implicate Kev Walsh. That was obvious to Toby at least. Nick was so cool, even though the two gendarmes were staring at him as he spoke. When they had gone Mrs Taylor said she'd like to speak to Toby and Lewis alone.

They had to go into the small staffroom with Mrs Taylor and Mr O'Kelly, after the others had been sent upstairs to their dorms. The quiz was cancelled. They needed to talk to them, Mrs Taylor said, because their names were mentioned in the letter. The anonymous writer had said 'Danny kicked Lewis and broke Toby's Walkman.'

She read from the paper Mrs Irons had given her. Elsa had obviously dictated the letter to her.

Mrs Taylor said, 'Did Danny kick you, Lewis?'

He said, 'Yes he did, actually.'

He told her about the playground incident, his version.

She said, 'Did he break your Walkman, Toby?'

Toby said, 'No.'

'But neither of you wrote the letter?'

'No.'

'And you don't know who wrote the letter?'

Lewis said, 'No.'

'Toby, do you know?'

He hesitated then shook his head.

Mrs Taylor said, 'Toby, why don't you want to be friends with Danny any more?' She was reading from the paper again.

He shrugged, because he couldn't trust his voice.

'But you were friends?'

'In the Infants.'

'But not now?'

He said, 'Our families are friends.'

She said, 'Well, you'll be pleased to know that the police are taking this very seriously. As you may know, they were criticised by the British press for not investigating thoroughly when an English schoolgirl was murdered in France. I'm not saying . . . ' She didn't finish her sentence and started again.

'But they don't want to make the same mistake twice. They want to see the original letter and are going to contact the British police. They are investigating this very thoroughly indeed. If you do think of anything, anything that might help, do tell us.'

She looked again at the paper in her hand. 'Your friends? They're Nick, Callum and George, aren't they, your dorm mates?'

119

They both nodded.

'We'll be speaking to them too.'

When they got back to the dorm Nick slung his arms round their shoulders.

'Well, what did you say, lads?'

Toby said, 'Nothing much.'

Lewis gave a fuller account and Callum said, 'You prat, Peters.'

He held up Toby's Walkman – in three pieces.

Nick said, 'That was a prattish thing to say. We told you to stick to our story.' He didn't like the turn events had taken.

There was a knock on the door.

It was Louise. 'Is Judas there?' She peered in at Toby. 'Your mother's on the phone.'

Through her braced teeth Rachel hissed, 'Fascist!'

Louise said, 'You're all Fascists. Don't think you'll get away with this.'

14

Nick came down to the phone with him, for moral support, he said.

Gilly Peters said, 'What's going on, Tobe?'

He couldn't tell her. The telephone booth had no door.

She said that Elsa was going frantic, had been ever since the anonymous letter. It had arrived that morning and she'd been on the phone straightaway. Toby's mum had persuaded her not to ring the centre till the evening. She'd told Elsa that the letter had most likely been written by someone who wasn't on the trip, Kev Walsh for instance, out of spite, because Danny had taken his place.

It was odd that she'd had the same thought as Nick.

But Elsa had been convinced Danny was suffering, even before she rang and discovered he was missing.

Toby's mum said, 'But the letter's not even true, is it? You took your Walkman with you. Danny didn't break it. You'd have said.'

Toby said hardly anything. It was hard to know what to say. Actually his mum's kind concerned voice made him feel like bawling. If Nick hadn't been there he'd have told her everything, even if it had resulted in a bollocking.

She said that Elsa wanted to come to France straight away with Danny's dad, but he thought they should wait a bit, and Toby's mum and dad agreed with him. They thought Danny might be making his own way home if he was unhappy.

She said, 'Was he unhappy, Tobe? Who would have written a letter like that? Have you any idea?'

He didn't answer and she said, 'Well, all I can say is, there must be some very nasty people at Lindley, much nastier than I'd thought. Anonymous letters are the pits.'

Shortly after that she put the phone down.

Nick slung his arm round Toby and kept it there while they walked up the grand staircase. When they got back to the dorm he said, 'The boy did fine.'

But shortly after that there was another knock on the door. It was Mr O'Kelly for Nick, Callum and George. The staff wanted to talk to them he said. They came back about ten minutes later, all three very confident. They'd all stuck to their story, even though they'd been interviewed separately.

While they were out of the room Lewis said, 'If we get the blame Toby Woby Worry Arse, it'll be your fault.'

Toby couldn't sleep. He couldn't stop thinking about Danny. He thought of creeping downstairs and telling one of the staff that Nick had written the letter, but when he got out of bed Nick got out too. When he said he was going for a pee Nick said he was too. Back in his bunk he thought that telling of Nick at this stage probably wouldn't help much anyway. He should have said something earlier. Much earlier. In the end he just prayed that nothing awful had happened to Danny. He wished Mrs Taylor hadn't mentioned that murder. It made him think of other things he'd read in the papers or heard on the news that had happened to more street-wise kids than Danny. Danny wasn't at all street-wise. He could be in all sorts of trouble.

Nick couldn't sleep either. He wasn't feeling as confident as he had looked. He hadn't liked the way Mrs Taylor had looked at him, or Kelly-O and he could hear Toby twisting and turning beneath him. Toby wasn't reliable. *He'd* got them into this in fact. He should have said Danny *had* broken his Walkman. Now – if the teachers discovered it was broken – they'd have to say that Toby had lied to protect Danny. But that didn't tie in with their fall back plan of blaming Toby if Toby split on them. It was obvious that Louise and Rachel blamed Toby already. But Louise had said, 'Don't think you'll get away with this,' to them all. It had got more complicated than he'd planned. What if the staff did believe Toby, who had looked weak and wobbly while talking to his mummy on the phone? Nick began to feel angry. Why didn't people do as they were told? Why hadn't Danny the prat managed to get back to the centre on his own? He'd learned all the proper phrases off by heart. The angrier he felt the quicker his thoughts came.

It was Danny Lamb's fault. He'd brought it upon himself. Everything had been fine before he came to Lindley. He ruined everything he came into contact with. He should never have been allowed to join their school. Should never have been allowed to come on the trip. He just wasn't a mixer. Mrs Taylor had said so. It was best if people like him kept out of things. That's why he'd written the letter. To help...

Suddenly Nick's thoughts came to a halt. He'd seen the letter in his mind's eye, on his shining computer screen – waiting to implicate him. What if his parents found out about all this? His father would *kill* him.

Rats in Lindley uniforms were chasing Danny. A rat with a face like Nick Tate's was close up...

'G-go away!'

Danny woke shivering and groped in the darkness for his bedside lamp. Couldn't find it. Couldn't find covers to pull over himself, only scratchy things. Then he remembered or half remembered though he couldn't see anything, but he could hear the wind whistling round his head and feel his foot hurting. And what was that other sound? It took him a few seconds to realise it was his own teeth chattering. He was cold too.

Eyes open.

He was in a black pit.

Eyes closed.

He was in a black pit.

It made no difference except that when he closed them the rat-face came closer, getting more and more like Nick's face the closer it came. So he tried to keep awake, but must have fallen asleep again, because when he next opened his eyes, the black was turning to grey. Here and there light was creeping in, between the tiles in a pitched roof. A rope hung from a beam above him.

'*Go hang...*'

Bad memories crowded in. Bad memories crowded out good. Cruelty crowded out kindness, because it was Nick and Callum's faces he saw in his nightmares, not Louise and Rachel's. In the distance a cock crowed as he remembered Callum pissing on him. He remembered them all pulling his clothes. Spitting at him. Calling him names, horrible names. He remembered being alone in the playground. Suddenly at five in the morning, the cold fact hit him. Raising sick in his throat. *Nobody* liked him. Not even Toby who had been his friend. He had walked away.

The cock crowed again.

He had no friends. For some reason no one liked him. They said he smelled, but everything about him was wrong. Everybody else had friends, but he would never have a friend. He was the *wrong material*. What did that mean? Wasn't he made of the same stuff as other people? Wasn't he flesh and blood? In the darkness Danny felt himself all over – he felt the skin on his hands and then on his face. He felt the nails on his hands, the hair on his head. He felt his eyes and long eyelashes.

Dan-ielle, do you smell?

Yes I do. I'm a poo.

Flush me down the toilet!

As the attic got lighter, Danny's thoughts got darker. His foot and now his head throbbed with pain, and he felt in his pockets for some painkillers. He wished he had some aspirin or paracetamol, a bottleful to put an end to all the pain for ever. But all he had in his pocket

125

was his Latin dictionary and a biro and a piece of paper.
It was the piece with the game of hangman on it.

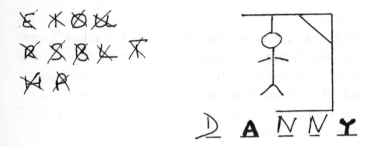

'*Go hang...*' Nick Tate had said. 'I'll show you the
rope.'

And the rope above him shook in a gust of cold wind,
disturbing a wasp which buzzed drowsily for a few
seconds.

15

Nick woke early and managed to talk to Callum, Lewis and Big George individually when they were in the bogs. He'd told them that on no account must Toby be left on his own, or he was likely to drop them all in the shit. Back in the dorm with Toby present, he said, 'Danny will turn up. He's sure to. He's got the whole French police force out looking for him.'

Nick had recovered his cool. His parents were unlikely to use his computer. They had their own computers. He'd probably deleted the letter anyway. He wasn't stupid. If Toby kept quiet things would be okay – whatever happened.

Toby had racked his brains half the night wondering what he should do. What could he do to help *find* Danny? Would telling the staff about the others – and about himself – help? The others were going to try and pin it on him anyway if things went wrong. *More* wrong. They'd gone wrong already. But he'd feel better if he told someone. Nick and the others obviously thought he might try. They were sticking to him like shit.

At breakfast Nick was all concern.

'Any news, Mrs Taylor?' She looked haggard and grey. Her tall frame sagged as she stood up to up-date them all. Danny hadn't been found, she said, but the police were getting a good response to an early morning television bulletin about his disappearance. They were hopeful. Danny had been seen yesterday. Today the police wanted the Lindley party to stay in the area. They wanted them to stick to their original timetable, while keeping in touch with the police. They'd given her a mobile phone. Danny might remember where they were going and try to join them. They must all keep a lookout, of course. It was Thursday, she reminded them. In the morning they were going to Arromanches, to the beach and to Arromanches 360, a circular cinema, where they'd see film of the landings. In the afternoon they were going to the Peace Museum at Caen. They would call at a war cemetery on the way. They might call in at a hypermarché on the way back – if they had good news. As she finished, Nick told Big George and Callum to hurry and get on the coach, to bag the back seat for the musketeers. He and Lewis stayed by Toby.

On the way to Arromanches Mrs Irons gave them a history lesson.

'In 1944 Europe had been occupied by the Nazis for four years,' she said. 'On June 6th 1944 – D-day – Great Britain and her allies put into action their secret plan to land on the Normandy beaches and drive the Nazis out of France. It was going to be their first step towards liberating Europe. Britain, a small country who had resisted Hitler's attacks, was determined to defeat the Fascist bullies!' She sounded quite impassioned, and someone started humming 'Land of Hope and Glory' but she didn't seem to notice. 'On the peaceful beach where you'll eat your lunch today, *thousands* of men died. Young men not much older than you gave their lives to free the world from fear! I want you to remember that,' she said.

As they drove along the coast road they could see the calm grey sea and the peaceful beaches. It was hard to imagine a battle taking place there.

Fascists. Fascist bullies. Rachel had called him a Fascist once, Toby remembered. Was he one? Fascists ruled by fear. Fascists despised the weak. Fascists persecuted anyone who was different. Blamed them for everything that was wrong. He looked along the back seat at Nick, Callum, Lewis and Big George who were all listening intently. Couldn't they *see*? What on earth had made him think he wanted to be friends with them?

Nick and Lewis stuck by him in the cinema where the circular film of the battle made it sickeningly real. You felt you *were* one of the soldiers as bombs exploded round you, planes swooped overhead and bodies fell at your side. It was a relief to leave at the end of the eighteen minutes. The real battle had raged for weeks.

Afterwards they ate their packed lunches on the very same beach, where all they could hear was the sea sighing and a few seagulls overhead. Then they went to a cemetery where the tidy lines of white gravestones stretched for miles it seemed. Nick and Callum flanked Toby as they walked between the rows, noting the names carved in the stone, and the ones without names. Some had just the word SOLDIER on them.

'It's so wrong!' they heard one girl say. 'We remember Elvis Presley's name, but what did *he* do?'

'Must have been shot to pieces,' Callum said.

Nick said, 'It must have been terrible.'

And Toby, thinking his conscience might have been touched, said, 'We've got to say something, about Danny I mean. It might help.'

But Nick shook his head. 'What's the point?' he said. '*You'd* get into such a lot of trouble.'

It began to rain and they made their way back to the coach.

Nick said, 'Don't worry. The police have probably found the prat by now.'

Danny read through what he'd written, on a blank page at the front of his Latin dictionary.

Dear Mum and Dad,
   I am sorry to do this to you
   but I can't stand it any more.
   It's hard to explain, but the poems might help.
   Love from Danny
P.S. Love to Jess too. Please look after Bunjy for me.

He'd written the poems in the back of the dictionary. He'd started them in class once. It seemed like ages ago. Everything was ready but he did want his family to know it wasn't their fault. He must try and make sure they got them. But what if no one ever came up to the attic again? It was afternoon already and the old man hadn't returned. He must have forgotten about him. What if no one found his Latin dictionary, with his poems inside? What if they never came up to the attic?

Danny had tried to open the trap door. But it wouldn't open – not from the inside anyway. Now he didn't want to open it. He didn't want to escape. There wasn't any point. He looked at his watch – half past two – and then through a gap in the floorboards. He saw a mouse below, eating flakes of baguette crust. Thinking he could enlarge the gap and drop the book onto the table, he started to pick at the wood with a rusty nail. Someone might come into the room below, even if they didn't come up to the attic. Then they would know what had happened.

16

The coach reached Caen, a modern town, most of which had been built since the war. As it drove down the wide boulevards past block after block of white flats, stained grey by the rain, Toby planned to break free from Nick and the others as soon as he could. In their company he'd become someone he couldn't bear. He hated them. He hated himself. But Nick and Callum kept close as they walked from the car park, up the steps, to the ultra-modern Musée pour la Paix. As he walked up the steps Toby could see their reflections either side of him in the glass doors. Henchmen. Minders. Big George and Lewis were close behind.

If he quickened his pace, they quickened theirs. If he slowed they slowed.

When he just glanced back at Louise and Rachel, who'd stopped to study the national flags flying high in front of the building, he felt Nick grip his arm.

Louise said, 'The Germans are our friends now, our allies. People can change. There is hope.'

Nick said, 'You're one of us, Tobe,' and steered him by the elbow.

And Nick gripped his arm as they queued for the main exhibition, on The Rise of World War II. All round them crowds of visitors were looking at displays or buying souvenirs from the huge gift shop. Several Lindley pupils wandered off to look at things or go to the loo, asking others to keep their places. But when Lewis said he was off to look at the Typhoon fighter on the other side of the foyer, Nick said, 'We keep together, right.' It wasn't a question and Lewis got back in line looking sulky. The five were in the middle of the Lindley part of the queue which was moving forward slowly.

The two women teachers were at the front, Toby noted. Mr O'Kelly was at the rear with Mr Bridges. He couldn't see Mrs Bridges. He wanted to get a message to one of them. How could he do that?

Shuffle shuffle.

At the front of the queue a door opened and Mrs Taylor and a few pupils went through.

Shuffle shuffle.

The door closed. The door opened and a few more people went in.

The floor sloped downwards.

The queue edged forwards.

And eventually they were at the front. The door opened and Toby, with Nick so close he could feel his breath on his neck, stepped into a dark passage, which seemed to move beneath their feet. It was like stepping onto a conveyor belt. There was no going back.

There were people in front and people behind so they had to keep moving. Too fast to stop, too slow to avoid seeing the stuff on the walls. Shuffle shuffle past spot-lit photos and documents showing events which led to the war. A photo of the railway carriage at Compiègne where the Germans surrendered after the First World

War. Shuffle shuffle. A copy of the Treaty of Versailles which humiliated and isolated them. Shuffle shuffle. A queue of unemployed with haggard faces. Shuffle shuffle onto the next one whether they wanted to or not.

Hitler, a small figure addressing a rally.

Hitler, a bigger figure addressing a bigger rally.

And a Jewish girl wearing a yellow star.

A bigger rally and a bigger Hitler. People cheering and Jewish people leaving their homes.

Jewish people being herded onto trains.

And a bigger rally and louder cheering as Hitler made German people feel better by blaming the Jews for everything that was wrong – unemployment, inflation, poverty and illness. Now they seemed to be hurtling forwards as the passage spiralled downwards, and suddenly they were in a room transfixed by Hitler's manic face pulsating with electric blue light.

A girl said, 'Oh my God! A descent into *hell*!'

And the word echoed – hell hell hell – in a computery sort of way round the empty room. For there was nothing else in it, just the blue light and Hitler's mesmerising gaze. It seemed ages before someone started moving again. Then they all stepped into another room where they found themselves face to face with the life-sized photographs of a boy and girl.

And they *were* in hell. The boy had a noose around his neck. So did the girl.

A caption beside the photograph said:

Aged 15 and 16, photographed just before they were hanged.

There were more photos round the room of people in concentration camps. Hundreds of people with hollow faces like skulls. Toby had read Anne Frank's diary. Now, he realised that there were hundreds of Anne Franks. Thousands of Anne Franks.

'I wouldn't want to meet him on a dark night,would you?'

Someone was *joking*. Toby looked round and was relieved to see most people were shocked. He saw a boy from 7X with tears in his eyes. Then he heard Lewis giggling. 'I put our game of hangman under prat's pillow.'

Toby slid from the room. Then he ran zig-zag through the crowds. Out of one room into another. Past horror after horror. Glad he couldn't stop to look. From prison to gas chamber. From gas chamber to battlefield. From battlefield to concentration camp. This way and that, praying he'd come to an exit soon. Into a dark room lit by candles, one for every thousand people who'd died in concentration camps. *Hundreds* of candles. *Hundreds of thousands* of people. Into a cinema showing another battle. Into a brick wall, part of a street of some old city with swastikas on the walls. Down an alley. Into another street with people wearing yellow stars. More swastikas. Dark dark dark. And sick sick sick of all the misery in the world, and desperate to reach the exit, Toby pushed a door and – he'd found it – the exit. At last he was in the foyer. Light! Bright light! Blinking, he took his bearings. Typhoon to the left. Gift shop to the right, Toilets beyond. No teacher in sight, but none of the gang either. Feeling in his pocket for a pencil he crossed the foyer and headed for the lavs.

Dames. Messieurs.

Cubicles – good – and a sit-down lav.

Seconds later he was writing on toilet paper.

You've got to find Danny quick.
He's in danger. He might DO something.
We've made his life unbearable. ME and the others.
Lewis told him to hang himself.
Nick wrote the anonamous letter.
Toby Peters.

He stuffed it in his pocket. Now what? Give it to a teacher as soon as he saw one. On the bus if not before. Or even one of the museum officials. Or a gendarme. The first adult he came to. He could explain it was about the missing English boy. There might not be much time.

But as he came out of the cubicle, the door of the next one opened. Callum pushed him back inside. Nick pulled the letter from his pocket.

'You can't give anyone that, Tobe, the spelling's all wrong.'

He threw the letter in the lav and flushed it. It wouldn't go down. They made him fish it out with his hands and tear it into pieces.

'We should make him eat it.' Big George was there too.

Lewis giggled.

Nick said, 'It was a mistake, Tobe. You won't make a

mistake like that again, will you?'

Callum punched him in the stomach. He doubled up with the pain.

Then they heard Mr O'Kelly saying, 'Anyone from Lindley High here? If you are, hurry to the coach please. We've got to go straight back to the centre.'

But he didn't come in.

Nick called out, 'Coming, Sir!' And flushed the lav again.

17

Nobody took much notice when Toby was helped onto the coach by Nick and Big George. Mr O'Kelly was standing by the door marking people off the register as they arrived.

Nick said, 'He's a bit upset, Sir, and he's got a gutache.'

Mrs Taylor was standing at the front, trying to get her mobile phone to work. As they moved towards the back they picked up what had happened from what everyone else was saying. In the museum Mrs Taylor had had a phone call from the police telling the party to return immediately. She'd said, 'Have you found Danny? Is he all right?' several times – but the phone had gone dead on her.

Toby, who was crying, sobbed even more.

As they passed Louise and Rachel, he heard one of them say, 'Guilt obviously.'

Someone said, 'His mates are as bad. Nick Tate's a nasty bit of work, I've always thought.'

Nick pushed him onto the back seat, muttering, 'Stop blubbing. Pull yourself together. Just keep quiet, okay.'

Nick was trying to keep a cool head. Toby seemed to have lost it completely. Nick didn't like the way things were going. But if Danny Lamb was dead – as some people clearly thought he was – *it wasn't their fault*, and at least he couldn't give evidence against them. So all they had to do was *keep quiet*. If Danny was alive and blamed them for the bit of teasing they'd done, they'd deny it. If Toby insisted on blaming them, then they *four* would all blame him. If Toby said anything about the letter, all four of them would say that Toby had written it. It would be his word against theirs.

He said, 'It's in your *own interest* to keep quiet, Tobe. Shut it.'

But the prat carried on snivelling. Fortunately he wasn't the only one crying so nobody took much notice.

As Ted started the engine, Mr O'Kelly made a speech, saying they mustn't jump to conclusions. They mustn't fear the worst. They didn't know yet. Danny may have turned up alive and well. Mrs Taylor was still trying to get back to the police but they were in a low-lying area and the mobile phone wasn't working very well. It took them half an hour to get back to Brion sur Mer.

When they arrived at the UNCMT, Mrs Taylor got out and Mr O'Kelly told them all to stay in their seats. Nick noted a grey 2CV, a black Renault and two police cars in the drive and a gendarme on duty at the door. When Mrs Taylor fired a round of French at him, the gendarme nodded curtly and pointed inside. She went in and it was a good five minutes before she re-appeared in the doorway. Mr O'Kelly went out to her, and then came back saying they were all to follow him into the activities room where an announcement would be made.

What was going on? Nick tried to study the teachers' expressions and saw glances passing between them. But what did they mean? He'd never seen Kelly-O look so stony before, almost as stony as the gendarmes who never smiled. It was a bit unnerving. As he stepped off the coach, Nick tried to catch his eye but didn't manage it. Kelly-O chivvied them along as if they were infants. Then he made them line up outside the activities room where Mrs Taylor was waiting with the older of the two gendarmes who had visited yesterday. He was still smoking.

Mrs Taylor said, 'Will you all go in now, filling up the seats from the front?'

The five were near the back of the line. Nick and Callum 'helped' Toby who was still blubbing. Nick managed to mutter, 'We just keep quiet,' to Lewis and George but that was all. There was a shout of '*Silence!*' in French from the gendarme at the door, and another shout in English from inside the room. 'Silence. Complete silence, please!'

There was, they soon saw, a female officer at the front, directing operations. She spoke English very well.

The room had been re-arranged. Five rows of chairs faced the front where there was a screen and an overhead projector on a long table. Their model and displays had been pushed to one side. Behind the table sat a white-haired old man and a boy about their age. At first glance most people thought – or hoped – the boy was Danny, though this boy was dark with rimless glasses and looked nothing like him, except for a slight touch of the professor in his manner.

Nick found himself on the back row with Toby and Callum and Lewis and George and a couple of nonentities from 7X.

Mrs Taylor came in and closed the door, then stood behind them at the back. Nick straightened his back and looked straight ahead, as the female officer introduced herself as Commissaire Laclos. She asked them all to listen carefully.

Everybody was listening. The silence was total.

'Your friend, Danny Lamb, has been found in very sad – and suspicious – circumstances,' she began. 'It is our duty to investigate this matter very thoroughly. We will in due course be interviewing everyone in the room, but first I want you all to listen to Leon Claude, a boy of your own age. Leon found Danny.'

The boy sitting by the old man stood up. In good but accented English he said he was the grandson of Leon Claude, a hero of the Resistance, and he had found Danny in his grandfather's deserted gîte. The old man, presumably the boy's grandfather, nodded, and the boy went on.

'I found Danny,' he said, 'in ze attic. And zis. I found zis.' He held up a book. Toby recognised it immediately. It was Danny's blue and white Latin dictionary 'And zis,' he said, holding up a scrap of paper. Only the first few rows could see that it was a game of hangman.

But someone clicked on the projector and there was a gasp, as the image appeared on the screen.

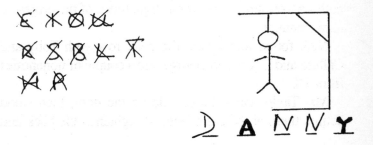

Toby closed his eyes.

Nick looking down at his own hands was surprised to see them shaking.

The projector hummed.

'There is somezing else,' said the boy.

Click. Click.

The something else came onto the screen.

Toby kept his eyes shut.

Nick sat on his hands and felt his heart thumping in his chest. Keep calm, he told himself, keep calm. For a feeling he didn't recognise was welling up inside him.

'You can all read zis, yes? You are 7Y, yes?' said the boy.

Reluctantly Toby opened his eyes.

Nick kept his eyes on the screen.

7Y

Why did you hate me on first sight?
Why did you follow me home at night?
Why did you jeer?
When I came near?
Why did you spit?
Why did you pull my clothes?
Why didn't you want to know me?
Why?

'Zis poem was at ze front of ze dictionnaire, wiz a letter,' said Leon.

Some people had obviously had enough.

A girl cried out, 'Tell us!'

Most people sat in stunned silence.
The projector double clicked again.
The words on the screen changed.

The Week
On Monday you stared.
On Tuesday you kicked my chair.
On Wednesday you called me sad.
On Thursday you hid my bag.
On Friday you pulled my hair.
On Saturday you made a dare.
Sunday I wasn't there.

Toby heard a howl, and wondered who it was, then realised it was himself. It was some time before he realised that another adult was speaking. And what she was saying. It was Commissaire Laclos.

'I repeat – *Danny is not dead but he is seriously ill. He hasn't committed suicide.* Leon arrived in time to prevent that. He saw the TV news flash about an English boy who had disappeared from the beach at Arromanches. He guessed what had happened – that his grandfather thought he was rescuing an English soldier. He informed the police, and he raced on his bicycle to his grandfather's old gîte. We know his grandfather who was a hero during the war. He hid British airmen at great risk to himself. He smuggled them away to safety. Sadly, now he slips into the past from time to time. Yesterday was the first time he had slipped so far. He now realises, and is devastated about what has happened. He insists that we investigate thoroughly to find out all the facts. He realises he could be accused of kidnapping Danny and trying to murder him.' She nodded at the French boy. 'Leon.'

The serious-looking boy continued.

'It was not my grandfazer who drove Danny to try and kill himself. I asked 'im why. I asked 'im who – and he told me. He showed me his poems. He told me everyzing. I zought 'e would never stop. He told me so many things. When 'e did I said, "And you are going to let zese Fascists *win*? Zis Nick..."'

Nick stared straight ahead though his insides were turning to liquid.

'"Zis Callum, zis Toby, zis Big George and zis Lewis,"' said Leon, looking at the back row. '"You must fight zem. You must *defeat* zem."'

Toby sobbed.

Lewis made a run for the door but was stopped by a gendarme.

Leon continued. 'I told Danny 'ow the Fascists tortured my grandfazer and cut off his zumbs. But that did not stop my grandfazer. I said *"Fascists must be stopped!"* Zen suddenly Danny became very ill. 'E is very red. 'E cannot breaze...' He mimed Danny struggling to breathe. 'Zen he fall. Fortun-ate-ly, les gendarmes arrivent. They give him ze First Aid. But he still do not move. I think he dead. They rush him to hôpital in ambulance.'

Leon sat down and his grandfather put his arm round him.

Commissaire Laclos said that Danny was in a coma. He was very ill but they did not know what the cause was. At first they thought he had taken an overdose of something, or that he had had an asthma attack, but they could find no evidence for that. Now only a life-support machine was keeping him alive.

'Wasp sting! He's allergic to wasps!' Toby managed to blurt out.

'In October?'

'Even a dead wasp could kill him!' Danny had told him all about it. *All* about it! 'He needs an injection of adrenalin! Quickly! He was supposed to carry it with him at all times. It must have been in his lost bag.'

Mrs Irons sprang to her feet saying it was true. She remembered now. She'd got everyone's medical details. A gendarme rushed to the phone.

It was vital information, he said when he came back. The doctors were very grateful. It gave Danny a chance. Now all they could do was wait. In the meantime, Commissaire Laclos said, the police would begin their interviews. They would start with the students on the back row.

The old man held up his hand and began to speak slowly in heavily accented English. 'I want to tell you, all of you, you must fight Fascism wherever you find it. Above all *you must fight ze Fascist in yourself.*'

Nick felt the old man and the French boy staring at him. The gendarme at the front was staring at him. Everyone was staring. He could feel eyes boring into his back. In

145

fact the police were looking closely at all the boys on the back row.

Nick thought – we just keep quiet, we just keep quiet. It was the idiot's own fault. He wanted to rally the others but couldn't. The idiot was alive, he wanted to say. Nick was relieved about that, he was. For some minutes he had thought he wasn't. The feeling that gave him was indescribable; it had taken him by surprise. He'd found it hard to keep a grip. But everything was all right now. What did a couple of poems prove? It was still his word against theirs. One against five.

'Why are you looking at *me*? We were just having a *laugh*!'

Nick shot a glance along the row. It was Big George blurting! Stupid oaf!

'It wasn't our idea,' snivelled Lewis. 'We just went along with Nick. He thought of it. He made us.'

'*He* dared him,' said George.

'And Nick answered the register.' Callum, sitting right by him looked at his feet as he spoke. Ganging up against *him*! Though Toby was still blubbing away, *proving* his guilt. They were all idiots. But they were not pinning this on *him*. He turned towards them.

'Lewis, *you* told him to hang himself, remember? You gave him the hangman game. You put it under his pillow. You told me so. He did, officer. We were in the museum. There were witnesses.'

He looked round at the rest of the class, but no one supported him.

Louise said, 'Shut up, Nick. Danny might *die*, don't

146

you realise?'

Commissaire Laclos had walked to the end of their row. She said, 'I must caution you all that anything you say can be used in evidence...' Then she led the five of them away.

18

Danny didn't die, but he didn't come home with the rest of the party. He had to spend eleven days in hospital before he was well enough to travel. His parents arrived later that evening.

Toby's parents came on the Friday. He told them everything and asked for them to come. When they arrived his mum and dad cuddled him and were very sympathetic. They told him not to blame himself too much. They told him that he had saved Danny's life by remembering about the wasp sting. They said that being Danny's friend had been a huge responsibility, too huge probably to bear alone. They should have helped more. That made Toby feel a bit better but not much. His parents made allowances for him. He hadn't *made allowances* for Danny.

It took Danny two months before he was well enough to return to school. It took Toby a long time to recover too – to stop hating himself. He didn't return to school that term. He needed to spend a lot of time thinking, and talking to people, before he felt strong enough.

The others – Nick, Callum, George and Lewis – got off scot-free some people said, because the French police said nothing illegal had occurred. But everyone knew something *immoral* had occurred and they showed it. That was painful for Nick especially. He had got used to being a star. But the worst thing for him was the thought of facing his father, who had been told. The Head of Lindley had been round to see all the families of those involved, Mrs Taylor said.

When Nick arrived back at Lindley High car park at just before nine o'clock on the Sunday evening only his mother met him. She stepped out of the darkness and picked up his bag and said, 'Hello, Nick,' but nothing else. She didn't speak to any of the other waiting parents. She didn't speak all the way home. He expected his father to be the same – to ignore him completely, for the rest of his life perhaps. Or go ape-shit, rant and rave, hit him even. What happened was worse.

As soon as he and his mum got in, Nick saw him, from the kitchen. He was in his book-lined study, slumped over his desk. His computer wasn't switched on. Nor was he reading. He just sat there with his head on his hands.

Beth Tate put the kettle on and said, 'Do you want a cup, Alec?' but he didn't answer. He didn't lift his head. His mum made the tea, put two cups on a tray and said, 'You'd better take this into him.'

Nick shook his head. He'd never seen his dad like this.

She said, 'Go *on*. See if you can get a reaction. He's been like that since Mr Jackman went this morning.' Mr Jackman was the Headmaster of Lindley.

So Nick went in and put the tray on the desk beside him, and after what seemed like an age, his father looked up. He looked dreadful. His three strands of hair hung down the wrong side, and his skin was red and puffy.

Nick said, 'Y-your tea. I've bought your tea.'

'Brought.' His father lifted a cup – with shaking hands – and drank. Then he turned and nodded at the other chair in his study. Nick sat down and his father swivelled round to face him. He could hear the kitchen clock ticking and see his mother standing in the doorway.

Suddenly his father said, 'Is it *my* fault? H-have I...' But he didn't finish. He just waved his hand at all the books in the room. Then muttering something about civilised values he started blubbing.

Nick didn't know what to do with himself.

After a bit he got up to leave. But his mum blocked the way. She put her arm round him and wouldn't let him shrug it off. She said that they had a lot to talk about. She said in quite a loud voice – it was as if she wanted his dad to hear too – that there was nothing wrong with crying. Then she said his father was ashamed because he thought he was a bad father. He'd failed to teach Nick civilised values like kindness and toleration. They had reared a clever thug, he said.

She said, 'Have we, Nick? Is that what you are? Or is there more to you than that?'

He didn't know what to say.

She said, 'You're going to need our support, Nick. Life won't be easy for you when you get back to school. If they let you back. This might mean expulsion.'

Then she let him go upstairs.

His mother was right. At school the next day, in the changing rooms before PE, Mr O'Kelly said quietly to Nick that he couldn't be captain of the team any more. He said he was sparing Nick's feelings and not making a big thing of it. He hoped Nick would learn to spare people's feelings in future. Then he got a note from the secretary saying he was no longer the 7Y representative on the school council.

And that wasn't the end of it. The Danny Question as it came to be known, was the question for the rest of term. They discussed it a lot. No pupils or staff were allowed to deny or forget their part in Danny's suffering. Or his happiness, because he had had some good experiences at Lindley thanks to a few people. Everyone had to consider The Danny Question. How do we treat people who are different? How do we treat the Dannys of the world? Like lepers of old? Like blackbirds with white on their wings?

Danny never did go back to Lindley. When he was well his parents moved him to another school, a small private school. It claimed to have a caring policy and Latin lessons for everyone. Toby heard that he was okay there. He hadn't made any close friends but he hadn't made any enemies either. Some people at Lindley were disappointed that Danny didn't return to their school. They wanted a second chance to prove they could do better, but Danny and his parents didn't want to take that risk.

Toby did go back, but not till January. There was a sprinkling of snow on the playground when he walked in. Otherwise it looked as he remembered. Or did it?

There were the usual groups round the sides trying to look cool. Mr Hall was stamping his feet to keep warm as he talked to a couple of girls. An informal footie match was going on in the middle with the usual players, except that Nick Tate wasn't in the middle of the fray. Nor was Callum Nolan. He had gone to Scotland to live with his dad, he'd heard.

Toby had heard about Nick losing his captaincy but hadn't expected it to affect the playground games. Where was Nick? He looked all around. Then thought he must have left too, till he saw a solitary figure on the edge of the playing field near the spinney. Was that him? Surely not?

The bell rang.

When Toby walked into 7Y's classroom the first thing he noticed was that Mrs Dempsey was back, shouting, 'Order! Order!' Then, that there were three spare seats, two at an empty desk behind Lewis and Big George, who were still the class twits it seemed. They were mock-fighting with rulers.

The other was by Nick who sat at the front alone. And there was a space round his desk, as if a ring had been drawn round it. He was reading a book. People were ignoring him completely.

Mrs Dempsey said cheerily, 'Hello, Toby. Welcome back. Where are you going to sit now? You've got a choice, see. Danny Lamb's transferred as you know, and Callum's gone back to Scotland.'

Toby thought hard for a few moments, and then he went and sat by Nick.

Author's Note

The starting point for this book – and all my books – is 'real life'. To write it I talked to lots of children and adults about their experiences. I would like to thank them for all their help, and sometimes their painful honesty. I also collected data from the media. Then I used my imagination to create the characters, setting and plot. As always I used a mixture of real life and imagination to create a fiction which tells a truth.